The Baron in France

Inside the safe were jewel cases.

He took several out, carried them to a wooden crate, opened them and began the search. There were jewels here he had neither seen nor heard of; beautiful gems. He felt their almost magnetic attraction; he wanted to study them, examine all their beauty. That was always a danger—that the brightness and the beauty of diamonds, above all others, would fascinate, almost hypnotize him, and destroy his judgment.

He went through case after case, and did not see the Gramercy stones.

There were three cases still unopened. He did not trouble to take these to the crate, but opened the first where he knelt; and the first diamonds which scintillated up at him were the Gramercys. He hadn't a moment's doubt.

Other titles in the Walker British Mystery series:

THE BARON IN FRANCE
John Creasey
as Anthony Morton

WALKER AND COMPANY · NEW YORK

First published in the United States of America in 1976 by the
Walker Publishing Company, Inc.

This paperback edition first published in 1983.

ISBN: 0-8027-3001-9

Library of Congress Catalog Card Number: 76-24558

Printed in the United States of America

10 9 8 7 6 5 4 3 2 1

CONTENTS

I

THE MURDER

The man at the safe worked swiftly but without haste. His hands, the fingers tipped with adhesive plaster, manipulated the tools deftly, easily. It was an old safe. It would have been quicker to blow it; but that would have roused everyone in the flat and most people in the building.

The burglar worked on . . .

Light from a torch with a large broad beam shone on the black safe and the gilt lettering on it. The shadows of the man's fingers showed against it sometimes; or the exaggerated shape of a tool. The burglar made little noise.

A clock struck. One . . . two . . . three.

The man paused and stood up, looking at his hands. The palms were creased with sweat, the plaster at the tips of the fingers was dirty. He took a handkerchief out of his pocket and wiped his forehead, then walked across the room towards the window.

This flat was high up, on the third floor of the building —an old house on the outskirts of London, converted into three flats. The dark shape of a car showed just inside the gateway; so did the lawns and the flower beds.

Everywhere was quiet.

The man took out a hip flask, unscrewed the cap, and swallowed; swallowed again, and screwed the cap on firmly.

He took out cigarettes, lit one from a lighter, and then went back to the safe. As he bent down on one knee, the shadows of his hands appeared.

Metal scraped on metal; the dexterous twists of his fingers grew more rapid. The cigarette burned down and ash curled and then fell to the floor. Sweat beaded the man's forehead.

There was a sharp click at the lock of the safe.

He exclaimed aloud, in satisfaction; his eyes glowed.

He turned the handle and pulled; the door began to open.

He had worn a scarf over his nose and mouth at first, but that had dropped round his neck. He didn't pull it up, even now that he had finished smoking. He opened the door wide, and looked inside.

There were several jewel-cases, some wads of pound notes, bundles of papers, oddments. He took the notes and stuffed them into his pocket, then took out one of the cases and opened it.

The light seemed to increase tenfold; brilliance leapt into the room, fiery darts shooting out from the diamonds which lay against black velvet.

The man's eyes were aglow with excitement. He knelt there, staring as if the diamonds numbed him. The scintillating beauty blinded him to everything else until, suddenly, he closed the case—and it snapped.

He looked round at the door; the snap of the case had been too loud. But he did not need to worry. There was only the man and his daughter in the flat; and there was the whole width of the hall between the bedrooms and this room.

Only a fool would keep jewels like this in his own flat and in a safe made fifty years ago. Dealers *were* fools.

The burglar was grinning; nervous tension gripped him.

He opened four more cases; there were rubies, emeralds and sapphires, but no more diamonds. He did not linger over the other stones, but slipped each case into a pocket; all his pockets bulged.

He began to collect the tools and stuff them into a canvas roll, lying unrolled on the floor in front of him.

The clock struck the half-hour as he picked up the roll and began to fasten it round his waist.

The door opened.

In that swift, bewildering moment, light flooded the room, shone on to the burglar's face, showing every feature clearly—good features in a pale, startled face. In the doorway stood a man, wearing pyjamas, carrying a poker.

The tool-kit dropped to the floor.

"That's stopped your little game,'" the newcomer said. His voice was hoarse, his hair dishevelled, his grey eyes looked very bright. "Stand up!"

The burglar stood up by the side of the open safe, his foot touching the tool-kit. The other man moved forward, raising the poker.

"Turn round, and——"

The burglar dropped his right hand to his pocket, and snatched out a gun. Some jewels fell as he did so. The man in the doorway leapt forward with poker raised. The gun roared; twice. Bullets tore into the chest of the man with the poker. A foot away from the burglar, he stopped, reared upwards, and clutched at his chest. He made funny little sounds deep in his throat. Blood appeared between his fingers.

He pitched forward.

The burglar moved back, to avoid his victim's body. He thrust the gun into his pocket, snatched up the kit, and peered round. He ignored the small jewels on the floor. His eyes looked different, his manner was different; there was fear in him. He saw nothing that he'd dropped, and tried to think. Now, he'd tidied everything up. He could——

A girl screamed.

The sound tore through the burglar's body much as the bullets had torn through flesh and bone. His heart gave a wild leap.

The girl was in the hall. Obviously she had just crept there from her bedroom. She was small, and very young; twelve, he knew. She had long fair hair and wore green pyjamas which were too small for her. Her enormous eyes looked like pools of blue flame.

She screamed again.

The man snatched at his gun, but fumbled. His movement, perhaps his expression, galvanized the child into action. She sprang towards another door—the door of the flat which led to the staircase—and disappeared.

The man leapt forward, but kicked against the outstretched hand of the man he had shot. He tripped. He was frightened and had lost his nerve. He banged against the room door, and hurt his knee and his hand.

Another door slammed.

The man rushed forward, swearing viciously. The landing door was closed. He hurried forward and opened it, and heard the girl running down the stairs and screaming:

"Help! Help! Help!"

The man thought he heard another sound, of a male voice. He stopped, swung back into the room, and closed and locked the door. Then he went to the window out of which he had looked at three o'clock. Nothing had changed; the dark shape of the car, of the lawns and flower beds, all were there.

He flung open the window, and began to climb out. There was a rope, hanging down; and nearby were drainpipes and window sills. He went down, holding on to the rope, which he had fastened on to a drain-pipe earlier, to meet such an emergency as this. He held on to the rope with both hands, and kept his feet against the wall.

Half-way down, a light flashed on from a window near him.

It fell on to his face, and there was nothing he could do about it. He actually saw into a room. A man was getting out of bed, naked except for a pair of pyjama trousers. A woman, her dark hair tousled, was leaning up on one elbow. Her mouth was open.

The man went out of the room.

"Fred!" the woman cried.

The burglar did not think she had seen him. He went on down as swiftly as he could, and reached the ground. He stood quite still for a moment, fighting for breath.

Lights appeared at other windows.

The burglar took out his gun and held it tightly as he went towards the little car, which was pointing towards the road. He made no sound as he got in, and didn't close the door properly; it needed slamming. He started the engine. Then he thought he heard a shot, but couldn't be sure. He eased off the brake, the car nosed towards the road. Once on it, he trod on the accelerator, and swung towards the right, the main road, and London; the easiest city in the world to get lost in. The engine roared. He didn't look out or upwards, or he would have seen faces at the windows of the flats.

Inside, the man wearing pyjama trousers was on the second floor landing, with a neighbour from the bottom floor, and the girl. She had stopped screaming, but was shivering uncontrollably. The men couldn't get a word out of her.

The tousled woman reached the landing, took the girl in her arms, and said:

"Betty, don't worry, tell me what it is."

The girl shivered and shook, and there was horror in her eyes. She did not attempt to speak.

"I don't like this," one of the men said.

"Go and find out!" screeched the woman. "Go on, Fred!"

The two men, one with a dressing-gown on, started upstairs. On the top landing was the closed door, and nothing to guide them. They put their shoulders to the door, and it creaked; at the third attempt, it swung open.

Lights were on, and the shot man lay crumpled up on the floor, lying in his own blood.

"Look—at *that*," Fred said huskily.

"He looks——"

"Better dial 999," said Fred, hitching up his pyjama trousers. "I'll see if I can do anything for him."

He went towards the fallen man, and knelt beside him. He touched the outflung arm and hand, but it wasn't necessary to move the victim. Death spoke silently. He heard the ting of the telephone bell, and the dialling sound, and then his neighbour giving the address—Old Manor, Rickham, Surrey. The bell tinged again. The neighbour turned towards him.

"They're coming. Is there——" he broke off.

"Not a hope," muttered the man named Fred. "Must have been instantaneous. Ghastly business. Ghastly for— that kid downstairs."

Downstairs, Betty was still shivering, although now she lay in the neighbour's bed, with clothes piled on her. The distracted woman with tousled hair tried to make her talk, tried to drive horror away.

2

JOHN MANNERING

JOHN MANNERING lay in bed. . . .

He felt lazy and disinclined to stir. He had good reason. His wife sat at the dressing-table, combing her hair. It was long, lovely hair, black and with a sheen which made it beautiful. Here and there were grey strands, but they were lost in the mass of black.

She sat sideways to Mannering.

She wore just a wrap; it covered her creamy shoulders but fell away from her breasts, and she was not disturbed although she knew that Mannering was studying her. The slow, steady movements of her arms and hands fascinated him. So did her face. Her features were smooth and regular; her skin was a little dark, not quite sallow; her smile was almost sultry. There were those, who did not know her well, who called Lorna Mannering aloof.

"Darling," Mannering said.

"You should be up."

"Impossible," said Mannering, and grinned. "You should be here."

"It's after eight."

"What makes that a crime?"

"You have to go to a sale."

"Larraby can go," said Mannering. "Why should I pay out huge salaries and do the chores myself? Darling, I can't be quite sure, but I think you're the most beautiful woman in the world."

She stopped brushing, and made a face at him.

"Of course if you'd prefer me to *make* sure——" he said hopefully.

The telephone bell rang.

They both glanced at it, on the bedside table. Lorna stood up. Mannering watched her, and the telephone rang again. She pulled the wrap round her shoulders and held it together in front. He grinned, turned and stretched out for the telephone.

There was no reason in the world why this should be bad news. The thought did not enter their heads.

"John Mannering here."

He listened, and frowned. Lorna's expression changed, because of something that happened to him. All sign of laziness had gone. He looked younger, different; somehow, sharper. She knew that she was married to two men in one; John Mannering her husband and her lover, and John Mannering whom the world had once known as the Baron, and who at times was still the Baron and all the things that meant.

"Yes," he said quietly. "Yes, I'll come. At once."

He rang off, and looked at Lorna. The change was complete. His hazel eyes had been laughing at her just now, filled with the gaiety which was part of him; all laughter had gone. Lorna knew what it was like to see an eagle, swooping. He often reminded her of the eagle.

"What is it?" she asked.

"Bernard Dale was shot and killed last night," Mannering said. "His safe was emptied. His daughter's in hospital, suffering from shock." He was already at the door. "He was with me yesterday afternoon, probably had the Gramercy jewels in his safe."

Mannering disappeared, into the bathroom.

His wife turned towards the mirror and looked at her reflection, and saw that she had changed too. The happiness faded from her eyes. Something like fear replaced it.

She had often known fear, because of Mannering.

In their early days, it had been because of the devilry in him; the streak that some had called bad. While police and press and public had screeched hatred for the Baron, that jewel-thief extra-ordinary, she had come to know that the man she loved was the Baron.

Press and public had gradually changed their tune; began to tolerate, then to admire, finally to turn him into a kind of hero.

Looking into that mirror was like looking at the years as they stood in marshalled array, ready for inspection. First a rich man had been robbed by the Baron; next a dozen poor men were dazed by gifts.

Even now, Lorna could hardly believe how the stories of the Baron had spread; how he had captured the imagination of the millions; how he had managed to appear to them almost as a public benefactor.

All that had changed in time, too.

She had helped to change him. Thanks to her, he had "settled" and bought Quinns, his shop—of its kind the most exclusive in the world. But the deep core of daring and courage, some quality which had always been in him, kept rising to the surface. He could have set up a brass plate at Quinns, reading: *John Mannering, Private Detective*, and been assured of more work in a month than he could handle in a year. As it was, he handled few cases, was only moved to take one by some deep personal motive.

He knew Bernard Dale well.

Occasionally Mannering was consulted by the police; few men knew more about precious stones, especially the old and famous gems. There was even a Superintendent at Scotland Yard, Bill Bristow, who knew that Mannering was the Baron, had never been able to prove it—and whom circumstances sometimes turned into a fellow investigator.

Lorna knew that Mannering wouldn't be thinking about Bristow, now.

He would be seeing the greying hair and the pleasant face of the murdered man.

Lorna went into the kitchen. She put bread into the toaster, made tea, prepared a dish of cereal. Mannering liked a cooked breakfast but wouldn't wait for one that morning,. even if Lorna cooked it herself. Their maid was away.

Lorna was quite sure what was in his mind: swift desire, sudden longing, to find the killer.

He came in, freshly shaved, fastening his collar, with his tie draped round his neck.

"Hallo, my sweet! I'm ready for a snack, too." He kissed her lightly on the cheek as he sat down. "Thanks."

"Who called you?" asked Lorna.

"Bristow."

She didn't comment, but poured out tea. He took it, talked a little, mechanically, glanced through the letters which she brought from the front door of their Chelsea flat; but he was not really with her.

When he had gone she stood at the window of the large room on the top floor of this Chelsea house. He crossed the road, on the way to the garage not far off, but didn't turn and wave to her. Usually, he would have. Slowly she went back into the bedroom.

The watching years were heavy upon her.

A crowd surged about the house of murder when Mannering pulled up in his cream-coloured Jaguar. It was after nine o'clock, so there were no children. A uniformed policeman stood on duty at a white gate. The house itself was set in a large, well-tended garden, but was hardly a thing of beauty. Its grey walls and severe, late

Georgian lines, seemed to resent the sun which was shining from a cloudless sky.

Antirrhinums, asters, zinnias, all in a galaxy of colour, glowed in the flower beds; the lawns were trim; the gravel drive was neat. The front door stood open, and another policeman was on duty outside at the foot of the stairs.

As he approached, Mannering caught a glimpse of a man leaning out of an upstairs window.

The policeman on duty recognized him.

"Mr. Bristow's upstairs, sir," the second man said. "As far up as you can go."

"Thanks," said Mannering.

The first people he saw were newspapermen, all hurrying down. They stopped at sight of him, and a dozen questions were fired, all meaning the same thing. They were amiable and friendly, and three hurried on. The fourth stayed on the second landing with Mannering. He was a short, curly-haired man with a face like a cherub, whose name was Chittering, who knew a great deal about Mannering and suspected much about the Baron. He had a pair of the most innocent-looking blue eyes in the world; and there was no one whom Mannering would more readily trust.

"Officially consulted, John?"

"Yes."

"One thing about the old B, he doesn't let the grass grow under his feet," said Chittering. "Mind if I mention you?"

"I don't see why you shouldn't."

"Thanks. When did you see Dale last?"

Mannering's grin was taut. "I can't see any grass growing under your feet, either. Yesterday afternoon. Wait downstairs for ten minutes, and if Bristow doesn't object I'll give you a headline the others won't have."

"On your best behaviour, are you," Chittering mur-
mured. "I wonder how long you'll be prepared to wait for
Bristow's approval before doing what you want to do."
He grinned. "Hurry, John!"

Mannering went up the last flight of carpeted stairs
three at a time.

Another uniformed constable stood at the open door of
the flat. Several men were inside. Mannering saw them
busy, with tape measures, fingerprint powder, all the
routine of an investigation. If you were a policeman, you
had to work by rule of thumb, and it often got quick
results. Sometimes it took too long.

Two plain-clothes men nodded at him, no one else took
any notice.

He reached the door of the room where the safe had
been opened.

Bristow was bending over the safe, a man dressed in a
light grey suit, very spruce, with grey hair brushed well
back from a centre parting, his small, trimmed moustache
stained yellow with nicotine. A cigarette drooped from his
well-shaped lips. His grey eyes had an eager brightness;
he was in the middle fifties but looked little more than forty.

He glanced round.

"Oh, you've arrived," he said, without enthusiasm,
which meant that he was preoccupied; having sent for
Mannering he wouldn't mean to be offhand. "Won't be a
minute." He drew at the cigarette and it glowed very
red. "I don't know what to say," he said to the large,
bulky man dressed in brown who stood by him. "Forget it
for the time being." He took the cigarette from his lips,
then looked at Mannering, with his brows drawn together;
a deep groove formed between them.

Beneath Bristow the detective was Bristow the man.

"Thanks for coming so quickly, John. We've moved the
body. Have a look at these, will you?"

He turned from the safe towards a small table near the window. The sun shone through, here, and seemed to light a silvery fire at one side of the table. There was a little heap of diamonds, cut and polished but not set. Mannering saw these before he noticed anything else on the table, but there were various oddments including several legal documents, bank books, a small bundle of five pound notes, and some keys.

He did not touch the diamonds, but peered at them grimly. They were a fair size, and nicely cut, but there was nothing remarkable about them. Sold on the right market, they should fetch something like a thousand pounds each.

He took a pair of calipers from the pocket of his brown suit, and picked up a diamond, took it closer to the window, turned it this way and that; and fire seemed to strike from it as it caught the rays of the sun.

"Don't tell me that's a fake," Bristow said.

"It's no more a fake than you are," Mannering retorted, and gave the taut grin again. "*Are* you? These are new or recently cut and polished stones. If you really mean 'could they be big, stolen stuff cut down for resale?' the answer is yes—except for one thing."

"What's that?"

"They were found here."

"Hmm," said Bristow, and stretched out his hand for the calipers, picked up a diamond with them, and examined it in much the same way that Mannering had. "Not a hope of identifying them, anyhow. Are you particularly busy?"

"No."

"Have a look round first, and then we'll have a chat," Bristow said. "I'll want an inventory as soon as I can get it."

"Have you sent for his partner?" Mannering asked.

"Bennett? Yes, he shouldn't be long," Bristow said.

"Any objection to the Press knowing that Dale saw me yesterday afternoon, and took the Gramercy jewels away with him?" asked Mannering.

Bristow's eyes suddenly became frosty.

"*Did* he?"

"Yes."

"What are they worth?"

"Forty thousand pounds."

Bristow said, very softly: "How often did he deal in big stuff like that?"

"Whenever he had a buyer."

"How did he pay?"

"Cheque against delivery. I put it through his bank just before three yesterday."

"Who was he going to sell the stuff to?" Bristow asked.

"It was the one thing he didn't tell me," Mannering answered.

"Oh, was it." Bristow's eyes were half-closed. He stared at Mannering as if trying to make up his mind what to say next. He didn't smile when at last he broke the long silence. "Listen, John, no tricks. If you know who he expected to sell these to, tell me."

"He didn't say."

"And you didn't ask?"

"There's etiquette even in my business," Mannering said mildly.

"You'll have to teach me," Bristow growled. His eyes were wide open, now, and his gaze very direct; almost hostile. "Don't go off on a lone wolf act. I didn't know Dale had been to see you yesterday. I just wanted a quick opinion on those diamonds and anything else we may find here."

Mannering said: "I'll help where I can. What about this story for the Press?"

Bristow relaxed.

"You can go and unburden yourself to your friend Chittering," he said.

Mannering found Chittering in the hall talking to a youngish woman with a pale but startlingly attractive face, dark eyes, black hair which looked as if it had resented the brush and comb that morning. Her fine, dark eyes were slightly bloodshot, and she looked tired out.

"I just can't tell you any more," she was saying. "Betty's at the hospital. I didn't want her to go, but the doctor insisted. She doesn't remember a thing—it's the shock, he says."

"You've been very good," Chittering said. "Hallo, John. This is Mrs. Gorlay, Bernard Dale's neighbour from the flat below."

There were murmured courtesies, then Mrs. Gorlay went up to her flat; she had easy grace of movement and a figure which drew Chittering's gaze.

But Chittering was first and last a newspaperman.

"Any luck?"

"I sold the Gramercy jewels—diamonds, emeralds, sapphires and rubies—to Dale yesterday afternoon," Mannering said. "Their value, over the counter was at least forty thousand pounds. You could say that Dale bought them for a mysterious and unnamed collector who wanted them urgently, and who is going to be disappointed."

Chittering made a puckered O of his small lips.

"Name of said collector?"

"Not known."

"Clue Number One," said Chittering, and grinned. "I wish you luck, John! Anything else I can do?"

"Larraby or Carmichael at the shop will give you a history of the Gramercy jewels," Mannering told him, "and the more you print about them the more I'll think

of you. A good strong hint that we would like this collector to come forward would help."

" 'We' being you—or the police?"

"Regard us as one," said Mannering blandly.

"And butter wouldn't melt in his mouth," Chittering
jeered. He turned away, but didn't go far. "Wasn't there
some trouble between Dale and his wife a year or two ago?"

"Just divorce," Mannering said dryly.

"Odd circumstances, weren't there?"

"She ran off with a Frenchman, and Dale chased after
them."

"Oh, lord, yes!" Chittering rubbed the down on his
chin. There were moments when he looked no more than
a boy. "Nice time, that daughter of his is having."

Mannering shrugged.

Chittering went out, and Mannering returned to the
top flat. Bristow wasn't exactly waiting for him, but
seemed glad that he had arrived. He was sitting at the
desk, going through a book that looked like a diary. The
room, part living-room, part study, had a comfortably
homely air; armchairs were worn at the arms, everything
was planned for comfort rather than appearance.

"Now what we have to do is find out who Dale bought
those jewels for," Bristow said. "Sure you've no idea?"

"Not only that, I don't think he'll come forward,"
Mannering said. "Care to lay a bet?"

"No," Bristow said, and grinned. "But I think we'll
have an arrest within twenty-four hours. I've just had a
telephone call—Bennett, Dale's junior partner, was out all
night. His car has a bullet hole in the roof—and one of the
neighbours took a pot shot at the murderer. Like to talk
to him, when we get him?"

"Yes," said Mannering slowly. "I think I would."

Bristow noticed a change in his tone. "Now what's
on your mind?"

"I know young Tony Bennett well," Mannering said. "He's a nice lad."

"I've known a lot of nice lads get hanged," Bristow said dryly.

3

ARREST AND TRIAL

MANNERING sat in the small office at the back of his shop, Quinns, and studied the girl opposite him. She was in the early twenties. Some would have called her pretty, a few might have said that she was lovely. Now, her face was very pale, her eyes almost feverishly bright.

When he had seen her walking towards him along the shop, past the precious *objets d'art*, the treasures of the ages which made Quinns world-renowned, Mannering had realized that she was with child. He doubted whether she had many weeks to go.

She had come alone.

She was Hilda Bennett, wife of Tony Bennett, whom Bristow had arrested and charged with Bernard Dale's murder, three days ago. Mannering had seen her twice before; never when she had been so despairing as this.

"Sit down," Mannering said, and pressed the bell for one of his assistants to bring tea. It was the middle of the afternoon, and the day had been quiet.

He had found himself thinking more and more about Tony Bennett, about the evidence against him and the fact that Bristow was quite sure that he had the murderer.

Hilda lowered herself into a chair. A silver-haired man came in, with tea on a tray.

The girl looked as if she were going to swoon.

"It's no use, Mr. Mannering," she said. "I know you'll do your best. Everyone will. Dick's been——" she broke off, her voice suddenly hoarse, tears flooding her eyes.

"Dick's been wonderful. But they'll hang Tony. I've got an awful feeling that nothing can save him."

Mannering knew that the evidence was so overwhelming that it was frightening. If he told the girl that she was wrong, he might worsen the situation for her later. He could encourage faint hope but dare not go further.

"Bristow's thorough," he said. "And everything I can do, and the police for that matter, is being done. If we could be sure where Tony was that night——"

"We just can't," said Hilda, and closed her eyes. "I've told you just what he told me, Mr. Mannering. We were going to the pictures. Then someone telephoned him, said that he had a wonderful chance to buy some jewels very cheaply. You know what Tony is for business. He just dropped everything and hurried to Watford, where he was to meet this customer. He didn't tell me who it was. He'd been off on hurried trips like that before."

She paused.

Mannering passed her a cup of tea.

"And he was waylaid and drugged," Hilda went on. "When he came round it was early morning. He drove home...."

It was an odd, unconvincing story. The customer who was supposed to have telephoned Tony Bennett had been found—a jewel merchant with an extensive trade, who had a reputation second to none. He was emphatic that he hadn't telephoned Tony; that story was false.

It was possible that Tony had been to see another girl, Mannering knew; possible, but unlikely. He stuck to his guns, swore that the message had come from the dealer. The Watford police, Bristow and Mannering had tried to break the dealer's story; it just wouldn't break. The evidence that the dealer had not even been near a telephone at the time of the call was overwhelming.

"Tony assumed someone thought he'd had the jewels

on him," the girl went on wearily, as if she were reciting a lesson painfully learned. "He didn't want to disturb me, or worry me. He slept in the spare room. But there *was* the bullet hole in the roof of the car——"

Yes; his car had been used by the murderer; and there had been plenty of time for him to go to Dale's house and get back. He said he'd been forced to swallow a tablet which had sent him to sleep, but had not seen his assailant.

There could hardly be a taller story.

Dick Britten, Hilda's solicitor and a family friend, fetched her from Quinn's half an hour later. He looked as if he hated the task of trying to comfort her.

"I just don't believe that Tony did it," Mannering said to Lorna, a few days later, "and Bristow can yap from now until Christmas without convincing me. If they hang him——"

Lorna said slowly: "You're afraid that they will, aren't you?"

"I can't see a loophole," Mannering growled. "Tony knew the Gramercy jewels were at the flat. He had a key to the flat. He's a locksmith as well as a jewel-merchant, and he could have forced that safe. It's just a question of being sure that he shouldn't hang, yet not seeing a ghost of a chance of saving him."

"How is his wife?"

"I gather that she's almost prostrate." Mannering lit a cigarette. "Dick Britten will be here soon—he's with her now. He's having a hell of a time, too."

Britten, he knew, was Bernard Dale's brother-in-law; his ex-wife's brother. That had been characteristic of Bernard Dale—to be faithful and loyal to old friends.

"So Britten couldn't be busier," Mannering went on. He drew deeply on the cigarette and moved to the window of their Chelsea flat. He could see the shimmering waters of the Thames, not far away; and the stream of traffic along the Embankment. "She's in trouble all the way round. The jewels were under-insured. Bernard took a chance, didn't mean to hold them for long, obviously. The loss is big enough to smash the business. Nice outlook, both for Bernard's daughter Betty and for Tony Bennett's wife." He was pacing about. "I've never felt quite like this before—it's as if I'm being suffocated. There just isn't a lead to anyone else." He heard the front door bell ring. "That'll be Dick."

They were in the drawing-room, a lovely room of greys and blues; comfortable without being luxurious but in superb taste. They heard the maid walk across the hall of the flat, then a man's voice.

A moment later, the maid opened the door.

"Mr. Britten," she said.

Britten came in quickly. He was so fair that at moments he looked grey and much older than he was. At other times he looked absurdly young. Mannering had known him as a light-hearted, almost feckless young man with a little known serious streak in him. He was much more serious, now; an able man. His eyes looked tired, his shoulders drooped.

They shook hands.

"What will you have?" Mannering asked. "You look as though you could do with a double."

"Without much soda," Lorna said.

Britten forced a grin.

"You're about right. Thanks. I've spent most of the day with Hilda." He dropped into an armchair, and took a cigarette from the box which Lorna proffered. "Thanks again. I've also seen Tony. It's the most ungodly business, John. I *can't* believe that Tony did it, and yet the evidence seems to get stronger and stronger. The stuff which the defence digs up doesn't help. True, they haven't

found the jewels, but Tony had time to dispose of them—
could have had an accomplice, of course. I——" Britten
broke off. "Imagine how I feel about it. Bernard *was* my
brother-in-law, even if things didn't work out well." He
took the drink from Mannering. "Thanks. That word
keeps popping up! I've had Stella on the telephone from
the Riviera," he added abruptly, and tossed half the drink
down.

"Oh," said Mannering slowly.

Stella, now Madame Bidot, had been married to
Bernard Dale for ten years. She had run off—as the
newspaperman Chittering had recalled—with a Frenchman. Mannering had known her fairly well, but not so
well as he had known Bernard. She was a lovely creature;
if anything too light-hearted, too fond of gaiety, for her
solid, dependable first husband.

"She's badly cut up," Britten said. "More than I
thought she would be. What with Stella, Hilda and
Tony——" He jumped up, and whisky spilled over the
edge of his glass. "John, you've worked miracles before
now. Can't you see any hope? I don't give a damn what
it costs——"

"We don't need to worry about cost, either," Mannering said. "I've got everyone I know in the trade looking
for the Gramercys, or any jewels remotely like them.
Until we get some kind of line on them, we can't hope to
get a new one on the murder . The hell of it is——" He
broke off, glaring at the window as if the evening sky were
to blame for what had happened. "They might have
gone into a private collection and never see the light of day
for a century. They might be held under-cover for years.
Or they might be cut up into little stuff no one would
ever recognize. The chances of getting a lead through the
jewels before Tony is tried and convicted are so small that
I wouldn't give a pound for them."

Britten said: "That's what counsel says. We can't see an angle for the defence that will stand up. We'll try, of course, but there's hardly a hope. When Hilda realizes that the case is going on to the Old Bailey, I don't know what she'll do. I'm scared in case she kills herself."

Lorna said: "She won't; women don't." She gave a strained laugh. "I mean, we're tougher than you think we are, Dick. Who's with her?"

"Oh, her mother—she's all right from that point of view. If Bristow gets what he wants, I think the case will come up in about six weeks. The hell of it is when I think of a trial, I keep thinking of the verdict—and the hanging. It's haunting me."

Mannering said mildly: "You're taking it too hard." He refilled Britten's glass. "I can guess how you feel, though. The odd thing is that Tony says that he doesn't know whom Bernard bought the Gramercys for. If that's true, then Bernard kept a lot from his partner. I know we've been into all this before, but it still looks as if Tony's shielding someone. Think there's a ghost of a chance of that being the case?"

"I just can't make it out," Britten said hopelessly. "I don't mind admitting that I'd like to be given a job out of London for a bit. I know that sounds as if I'm shirking it, but I can't help, and——" he tossed the drink down. "What I want is a bit of gay life. I feel almost guilty at daring to say so!"

"You'll get over it," Mannering said. "How about cash?"

Britten said: "My firm isn't charging, of course. But we'll need a fat fee for counsel."

"Charge it to me," said Mannering.

He was not called by the Prosecution or the Defence, at

the trial which took place nearly seven weeks after Tony
Bennett had been arrested. Nothing new had come in;
and the evidence was overwhelming.

The Prosecution was as thorough as it could be, but
there was a curious calmness in Court, unlike the tension
in most murder cases. There was a feeling that the result
was a foregone conclusion.

The case lasted for a day and a half. The jury was out
for twenty-seven minutes, returned a verdict of guilty, and
the judge donned the black cap before he pronounced
sentence.

Tony Bennett, tall and powerful, stood and looked into
the old man's lined face, watching the pale lips move as
the fateful words were uttered.

Mannering also heard the words. He knew them well
enough not to be affected by the phrases themselves; but
Tony Bennett's expression bit deeply into him.

Tony had a round, good-looking face, curly hair, a fair
complexion and blue eyes which could be merry. When
meeting him first, the chief thought one had, was that he
was likeable. Everyone felt that; few had had a wider
circle of friends. It was something in his expression, in
the cast of his countenance, perhaps—and openness
which won everyone.

Yet none of his friends had been able to do a thing to
help.

In the dock, listening to himself being sentenced to
death by hanging, he looked incredulous. It wasn't that
he didn't understand, more that he could not believe that
it was happening to him. When it was over, he gave a
funny little shake of the head, as if he were rejecting the
very idea.

A woman in court began to sob. Another joined her.

Tony was led away.

Mannering left the court with Dick Britten. They

walked along the narrow street together, and at the corner on Ludgate Hill, Britten said abruptly:

"I can't face Hilda. Think you—think you could?" He jerked the words out.

Mannering said: "Yes, I'll see her."

Hilda was at a nursing-home in the West End. Her child, a son, had been born two days before the trial started.

Obviously no one had told her the news, when Mannering arrived. She realized intuitively why he had come, and what message he had to bring. She was alone, looking so pale and pure—as if innocence touched her, and horror had no place in her life. Mannering wished she would cry; but she listened and nodded and thanked him calmly. Afterwards, she behaved as if she were not made of flesh and blood; or as if the blood had dried up, and all her thoughts and actions were mechanical.

Uneasily, he left her, foolishly warning the matron and the nurses to be very careful.

He went straight to Scotland Yard.

Bristow was in his office, overlooking the Embankment. It was a long, narrow office, the leaves of the plane trees rustled close by the open windows. The sounds of traffic from the Embankment and from the river floated in.

It was warm enough for Bristow to be in his shirt-sleeves. The inevitable cigarette dangled from his mouth.

"Hallo, John, what's brought you?"

"You'll say idiocy. Bill, can you arrange an interview with Tony Bennett for me? I know I've no legal right, but you can fix it. I don't want to encourage him, or slip him a poisoned tablet or a razor blade!" Mannering forced a smile; that wasn't easy.

Bristow said: "I can see what's eating you. Everyone who knows him seems to feel the same. It's damned foolish sentiment. No one would feel like it if it weren't for the wife and infant." He offered cigarettes. "How do you think you can help him?"

"I don't know a way."

"I must say I expected you to make a damned nuisance of yourself before this," Bristow said, and then added with a rare rush of feeling: "And I half wish you had! But if you haven't been able to find anything to help him with, John, I'm damned sure no one else could." He paused. "All right, I'll fix an interview."

They met in Wandsworth Gaol, the following morning. Tony was already in the condemned cell. He wasn't dressed in prison garb. He didn't look ill—pale, perhaps, and thoughtful, but neither ill nor worried. His handshake was firm.

"Very good of you to come, John." They knew each other fairly well as fellow dealers. Tony and his murdered partner had called at Quinns once or twice most weeks. "I know you've been trying to work this thing out, but——" he gave a curious little laugh. "It's so silly. I didn't kill Bernard, you know. I can hardly believe that anyone in their right senses can think that I did. Silly is the word. Or—unreal."

There was a moment's pause; and then it seemed as if a glimmering of the real truth, of the coming horror, appeared before those blue eyes.

He gripped Mannering's hand fiercely.

"I can't believe they'll hang me!"

Mannering said very quietly: "Not if I can stop them, Tony. Now, listen. We *must* find out who Bernard bought those Gramercy jewels for."

"But I don't know!" cried Tony. "He didn't tell me everything—you know that. I was just the junior partner. He did a lot of work privately—secretly. Some of the biggest jobs went through without me knowing a thing about them until I saw the entries in the books. Even then, names weren't always mentioned. *You* should know how it is in the trade."

"I know," Mannering said.

He had felt a fierce surge, less of hope than of determination to find that missing proof. The surge died before this further proof of Tony's obvious ignorance.

"Of course, after Stella left, Bernard wasn't really himself, was he?"

"No. He was absolutely devoted to her. John, I can't believe any of it, you know. I don't just mean about the hanging." He moistened his lips. "I mean about Bernard. It's hard to believe he's dead. He was such a wonderful chap. I remember he came back from Chalon, after trying to get Stella to return to him. He talked to Hilda and me about it. I can almost see his face. He said: 'The trouble is, the fellow she's gone off with seems such a damned nice chap.' I mean, can you imagine anyone talking like that?"

"No," said Mannering. "No, I can't. Wasn't it—isn't it—a little-known dealer on the Riviera, named Bidot?"

"That's right. Raoul Bidot."

"He might be worth seeing," Mannering said.

That was less because he felt hopeful than because he had to give some slender hope.

4

REWARD FOR PATIENCE

MANNERING told no one except Lorna that he was going to
the Riviera. He was talking to Raoul and Stella Bidot at a
hotel in Chalon, a Riviera resort, late the following
evening.

He soon felt that it was a wasted journey. Bernard's
ex-wife did not seem happy, but Raoul Bidot was a gay,
smiling, handsome man with an air which would be likely
to attract any woman.

Mannering felt, as Bernard Dale had, that Bidot was a
"damned nice chap". But what about Stella? Now that
her first husband was dead, did she regret having caused
him so much misery? It was difficult to be sure; but there
was no doubt about her beauty.

Mannering flew back, still rejecting what seemed to
be inevitable. But the day of the execution drew
nearer.

He had never felt worse about a case; or felt that he had
not really started on it. From the beginning it had been
one damnable dead-end. Inwardly he was convinced that
the police were going to hang an innocent man.

He discovered that Bristow and the Watford police were
still making inquiries, that the dealer who was said to
have called Tony to Watford was still being watched. So
the police weren't really satisfied.

After a while, Mannering felt as Dick Britten had done
—he must shake it out of his system.

Ten days before the date of the execution, he took
Lorna out for the evening. His gaiety was brittle. Lorna

knew why, and did everything she could to help. But the evening had hardly warmed up before he seemed to forget that he was dancing with her.

"Darling," Lorna Mannering said.

"Yes, my sweet?"

"You're dancing with me."

"Oh, so I am," said Mannering. He moved his head forward and brushed her cheek with his lips. "The belle of the ball, or the despair of all debutantes!"

They were waltzing. It was not a ball but a night club which had become respectable and yet retained most of its patrons. In fact it was a pleasant place, where the food was good and the wine excellent and the service superb. Once a month, or even less frequently, the Mannerings came here. It was in Mayfair, where they could be sure of seeing someone they knew; and the purpose was to make Mannering forget a certain condemned cell.

"Who is she?" asked Lorna.

"Who?"

"The jezebel you're looking at whenever you can sneak a glance."

"Just a hag," Mannering said. "Whenever I really see you properly, I marvel that I ever look at another woman." He tightened his hold on her hand, and they laughed as they whirled about. He was very tense, all the same.

The dance stopped.

At their table, in a corner, Mannering lit a cigarette and murmured:

"Tall, red-haired, green-eyed, with the gilt dress."

Lorna looked about the room, at thirty or forty beautifully dressed women, their men in black and white. She saw the only red-haired woman there.

"I *see*," she said. "I suppose I shouldn't complain,

provided you continue to have such taste. She's really lovely."

"Thus speaks the artist in you," Mannering said. "Before long you'll be asking me to introduce you, so that you can suggest that she comes to Chelsea to sit for you. You'd do her justice, too."

"Darling," Lorna said, "is it my imagination, or do you lack a certain enthusiasm for her?"

"It's not your imagination."

"Who is she?"

Mannering hesitated.

Lorna saw something in his expression which she hadn't seen for two months or more, and would be quite happy if she didn't see for years. The last time, it had been when he had learned of Bernard Dale's murder; the same change came over his face, the familiar curiously brilliant look in his eyes, the eagle sharpness, were all there.

"Bernard Dale's ex-wife," he said. "Stella Bidot."

"No!"

"Without her French husband," Mannering murmured.

Lorna didn't speak.

"But with an elderly gentleman who hugs her tightly as if he dare not let her go," said Mannering. "Poor Bernard!"

Stella seemed to evade his eyes.

For Lorna, the evening had been ruined. Yet when the band struck up a quick-step, Mannering forced a grin, and asked:

"Care to dance?"

They danced, but it wasn't the same.

An hour later, Mannering opened the door of the cream-coloured Jaguar for Lorna, shut her in, then took the wheel. As he drove off, a couple appeared at the lighted doorway of the club, and he recognized Stella

Bidot, once Dale, and her elderly escort. Lorna saw his lips tighten; they said little on the way to Chelsea. The evening had heightened, not eased the tension.

They garaged the car and walked the hundred yards to the flat, in Green Street, near London's river. The stars were out, but it was late and there was little noise. That came from traffic on the roads somewhere far off.

Mannering opened the flat door and Lorna entered the spacious, carpeted lounge-hall. The other rooms led off this; and from one end of the hall a loft-ladder led up to the studio, where she spent much of her time.

"Nightcap?" asked Mannering.

"I think I'll have tea."

"In bed?"

"No, thanks," said Lorna.

She took off her wrap and put on slippers, then brought Mannering's from the bedroom to the study. This was a small room, with each piece of furniture old and valuable —and here only because Mannering liked it. Against one wall was an old oak settle, which deceived every visitor, for in fact it had been transformed into a modern, electrically operated safe.

Whenever Mannering kept jewels at the flat, he kept them there.

He brought in tea.

"Funny we should see the ex-Mrs. Dale," he said, and proved that the Dale murder was right on top of his mind. "There was a rumour that the Gramercy rubies had turned up a few days ago. Bristow asked me to have a look at them."

"And they weren't?"

"No. Slightly different dimensions and weights, but they were remarkably like them. I——"

The front door bell rang.

Mannering paused in pouring out tea. Lorna looked

round. Mannering put the teapot down, carefully, and moved towards the door.

"Odd," he said.

"It's been so peaceful lately," Lorna said, almost sadly. "I knew it couldn't last."

The bell rang again.

Mannering left the study door open, so that Lorna could see across the hall. He heard nothing as he turned the handle and opened the door. He was cautious, possessed an instinct nothing ever really killed. He kept his foot against the door, and could have slammed it in the face of the caller at the slightest threat.

A woman stood there.

He didn't speak; and that puzzled Lorna, for it told her how much he was surprised.

"Good—good evening," the woman said.

"Good evening," said Mannering at last, and stood aside. "Please come in."

A call from anyone would have surprised him at nearly one o'clock in the morning; a call from the ex-Mrs. Dale startled and puzzled him very much. But when he ushered her into the study, where Lorna was standing, he was poised again.

"Darling," he said, "I don't think you know Mrs. Bidot."

There was a strange tension in the room. The women were antagonistic, from the first instant. There was no doubt of Stella Bidot's loveliness, and her hair had a sheen which made it superbly beautiful. She was young, too; hardly more than thirty. Over the golden coloured dress she wore a black cape; over her head, a filmy scarf. She looked from one to the other, as if she didn't know what to say; as if she expected to find them hostile.

"Will you have a drink?" Mannering asked. "Or even tea?" He smiled.

She glanced down at the tea tray.

"No. No, thanks. I—Mr. Mannering, you *were* a friend of Bernard's, weren't you?" The words burst out, and she put a hand forward, as if in desperate appeal.

As if she didn't know.

"Yes."

"And—and when you came to France you did say that the police consulted you just after the murder, didn't you?"

"Yes," Mannering said again.

"Didn't you find *any* clue?"

Mannering said: "No. Does that really matter to you?" There was cruelty in the question. It hurt. He meant it to, not because she had antagonized him, but because he wanted to break down her tension, to find out quickly what had brought her.

"It matters a lot," she said, quite steadily. She paused, and sat down slowly. "I should never have left him. I blame myself for what happened afterwards." She stared at Mannering, seemed to forget that Lorna was there. "If I'd been there with him, then——"

"I shouldn't let yourself think that way," Mannering said, more gently. "It never helps to wonder what would have happened if you'd done this instead of that." He turned to the cocktail cabinet which was really a Jacobean court-cupboard, and poured her out a whisky-and-soda.

She took it without protest or comment, and sipped.

"Do you want to find the murderer?" she asked abruptly.

Mannering didn't speak.

"I think——" began the ex-Mrs. Dale, and then swallowed the rest of her drink. "Oh, I may be crazy but I think I know who it was!"

Mannering said, very softly: "Just guessing, Stella?"

It surprised Lorna that he knew her well enough to use

her Christian name; perhaps he used it now, just to try to ease that tension.

"Yes," Stella said, and caught her breath. "Yes, I'm just guessing." There was a wild look in her eyes. "Do you know the man I was with to-night?"

"No."

"He is the Count de Chalon," said Stella Bidot and caught her breath again. "An uncle of my—my present husband. You met Raoul. He's in Paris, his uncle had some business to do in London. I came to see my daughter, who is staying with Bernard's people. They've been very kind." The last words seemed to hurt her.

"People are," Mannering murmured. He didn't prompt her again; and Lorna poured out more tea, as if determined not to be affected by anyone's emotion.

"I think——" the woman began, and stopped. She fumbled with her handbag; Mannering thrust his open cigarette-case in front of her. "Thank you." She took a cigarette and then a light, and drew fiercely. "I'm only guessing, but I've got to tell someone! I believe Raoul's uncle has the Gramercy jewels!" Her eyes blazed suddenly, and colour burned in her cheeks. "*Do you see what I mean?*" she cried.

Mannering said: "Yes, I think I do." His voice was very gentle. "What makes you think he has them?"

"I heard him talking to Raoul's brother, Philippe. It was after you'd been to see Raoul and me. They seemed to think you might suspect that they had the Gramercys."

She looked distracted; as if she were suddenly assailed with doubts about the wisdom of talking. But she talked.

"Raoul's uncle, the Count de Chalon, has a big collection, and Raoul is a dealer. That's how we met. Two years ago, Raoul wanted some stones from Bernard. He said that they were for his principal. Bernard took me to the Riviera for a few days for a holiday while he did the business. That's when—that's when things went wrong between us." She caught her breath again, looked as if she were in torment. "I knew that Bernard was on the look-out for the Gramercy jewels at that time. He'd met the Count. The Count mentioned that he wanted them. You know—you know how a casual thing like that is said in the trade, don't you?"

Mannering said: "Yes, of course."

"I think Bernard bought them for him," the woman said in a choky voice, "but I can't be sure. I—I can't make up my mind what to think. Could Raoul have known anything about—about the killing? He——"

She broke off.

"Tell us everything, Stella," Mannering said, prompting her for the first time.

She bit her lips.

"I—I don't know whether I ought to say all this, I hardly know what I'm doing. Raoul was in England at the time of the murder. He'd left Chalon two days before, said that he had some urgent business to attend in Paris. He came back two days afterwards. I didn't think anything about it then, because he often went to Paris. But I found a London hotel bill in his pocket for those days! I was pressing his suit." She held the heel of her thumb tightly against her head. "I just don't know what I'm saying. I'm haunted by the thought that Raoul might have—might have done this. How can I—how can I go on living with him, if——"

She broke off.

"Why did you come here to-night?" Lorna asked in a brisk practical voice.

That was the tone that the other woman needed. She straightened up, looked into Lorna's eyes, and spoke more steadily.

"I've thought of going to the police—I had to do

something. Then I recognized your husband at the night-club. I was feeling dreadful. If I were right, then the man I was dancing with has the jewels that Bernard was killed for. Can't you see what a dreadful position it is? I can't *rest*——" she broke off, and closed her eyes. Then:

"I'm sorry. I'm not often as bad as this. When I saw you, Mr. Mannering, I decided to ask for your help. I thought if you knew all this, you might think of a way of finding out the truth." She glanced at Lorna, as if she realized that Lorna's answer meant as much as Mannering's. "Will you try? Will you?"

5

MANNERING ADVISES

THE woman's eyes burned and her cheeks were flushed; she gripped Mannering's arm so tightly that her fingers hurt.

"Will you try to find out?" she repeated hoarsely.

"I'd like to think about it," Mannering said quietly. He freed his arm and moved further away, poured her out another drink and mixed one for himself. "It's very hard to believe that if your uncle——"

"He's not *my* uncle, I detest the sight of him!"

"All right, if your husband's uncle had these particular stones," Mannering amended, "he would talk about them so carelessly."

"It wasn't careless. He and Philippe didn't know I was near. I crept away."

"I see. Did Bernard know that this Count who wanted the Gramercys was Raoul's uncle?"

"I don't think so. I didn't know myself until after I'd left Bernard."

Mannering said gently: "Why *did* you leave Bernard?"

"Don't ask me that!" she cried. "Don t ask me to explain why I was such a fool." She turned her tortured eyes to Lorna. "He seemed so dull, so prosaic. There was never any excitement, it was all work by day and quiet evenings, the radio, slippers, his pipe—oh, I revolted against it! Raoul was everything Bernard wasn't. The Riviera fascinated me, I hadn't been there before. It was a different world."

"How long was it before you started to regret it?" asked Mannering gently.

He ignored the glance which Lorna shot at him; the "don't make it worse for her" appeal.

Dale's ex-wife said: "Not very long. Three or four months. It isn't that Raoul turned against me, either, as soon as—as Bernard divorced me, we were married. I think he's still in love with me. It's just that I—I'm so hopelessly mixed up. Perhaps I'm dreaming that the Count has these jewels. But it's in my mind, like a constant nightmare. If I don't find out the truth I think I'll go mad! I can't help it!" she cried. "I can't sleep for thinking about it, I just can't rest. Raoul will soon know that something's wrong, and——"

"Hide it from him," Mannering broke in sharply. "Understand? If you want to find out the truth, hide your suspicions from him."

"That's easy to say, but——"

Mannering took her hands, and held them tightly.

"Listen to me," he said very quietly. "If you want me to help, you must hide your suspicions from your husband and his uncle. You must explain your nervousness away, feign illness, do anything you like but don't let either of them suspect that you think like this."

She didn't speak, but as she looked into his eyes, he thought that she realized what he really meant.

"I—I'll try."

"You must do it. How long is de Chalon going to stay in London?"

"Another few days. My husband is coming to-morrow, for two days. They want to see some jewels at Christie's," she added hoarsely.

"I see. How did you get here to-night?" Mannering wanted to know.

"By taxi. The Count took me to the hotel, and as soon

as he'd gone to his room, I came here. I just felt that I had to. I knew I shouldn't have the courage to see you in the morning. *Will* you help?"

"I will if I can find a way," Mannering promised. "What will happen if the Count discovers that you're not in your room?"

"Why should he find out?" Stella Bidot shrugged her shoulders. "I should tell him I went out for a walk, because I couldn't sleep. He——" her eyes filmed with tears. "I wish I could explain it all clearly. Until—until I began to suspect this, I quite liked him. He's fond of me, too. Now I hate the very sight of him. Whenever I see him I feel like shouting out about the jewels. It's almost the same with Raoul. If you can find out, tell me soon. I can't stand living like this, I just can't stand it."

Mannering said roundly: "I'm going to find out, but I can't tell you how long it will take. If you let them guess what's in your mind, I might never be able to do it." He gripped her hands again. "If they did kill Bernard, they might kill again. Do you understand, Stella? They might kill *you*."

She breathed: "Yes, yes. I understand."

Her taxi was still downstairs. Mannering paid it off, walked with her to his garage, and took the Jaguar out again. There was a chance, no matter how remote, that she had been followed.

He saw no sign of it as he drove her back to the Hotel Grand. He dropped her twenty yards from the entrance, so as not to be seen with her, and watched her go in.

No one appeared to take any interest in her.

He drove back swiftly through the dark streets. At the flat, Lorna was in the bedroom, in a dressing-gown.

"Sorry I'm late!" he said lightly.

"I thought you might go with her," Lorna said. "What happened?"

"No further incidents!" Mannering lit a cigarette and sat on the edge of the bed, looking up at her. "What do you make of the story and the lady?"

"She won't stand the strain for a week."

"No. It doesn't give me much time," Mannering said. "I'd better nip over to Chalon and see what I can find out." He sounded almost flippant.

Lorna said: "I suppose there's no point in saying: 'Must you?'" She hung up her dress. "All right, darling, I know you must. But what do you really think?"

"That if she's right she's in a lot of danger," Mannering said, "and if she's wrong she's probably heading for a mental breakdown. She believes it against her inclinations, against her will. She doesn't want to believe the Count and her husband or this Philippe are bad. It could be a form of self-deception, of course. Neurosis. Remorse at having deserted Bernard might have put the idea into her mind. Once it got there——" he broke off. "We'll see."

"You mean——"

"I mean," said Mannering carefully, "that I have suddenly discovered urgent business reasons why I should go to the Riviera! Face it, darling. Bristow couldn't do a thing about this even if Chalon lived in England. Getting help from the French police on the strength of an hysterical woman's story is out. But we've friends with francs in France!" He stood up, stubbed out the cigarette, and began to undress. "Coming?"

"Who are you going to tell?" asked Lorna slowly.

"Chiefly my wife," said Mannering. "Shall we fly or go by car?"

"We'll fly, and hire a car while we're there," Lorna said, "the Jaguar will be too noticeable." She moved across to him; quite suddenly they were in each other's arms. "But be careful, darling, be desperately careful."

He could feel the beating of her heart as she pressed against him.

Mannering felt more light-hearted, next morning, than he had for weeks. He could laugh at the idea of telling Bristow he was going; but he decided to tell Dick Britten.

Obviously there was nothing to tell Tony yet, and it would be cruelty itself to suggest to Hilda Bennett that there might after all be cause for hope.

He rang Britten, at his office, early next morning.

"Hallo, John," Britten said briskly. "How are you?"

"I'm fine. Dick, I think I've a line on the Gramercys. I'm going to try to follow it. Can you stand a shock?"

Britten didn't answer.

"You still there?" Mannering asked sharply.

"I—I—yes," Britten said, and there was a harsh note in his voice. "John, find those jewels. Find the swine who killed Bernard. If you can—if you can help Hilda——" he broke off, seemed to swallow his words, and then added with a brittle laugh: "That's the devil of it! It's not Tony I'm sorry for, it's Hilda. Tony's only thought is for her, too."

"Help the one, help the other," Mannering said tritely. "About Stella——"

"She doesn't come into this," Britten said abruptly.

"Good lord, no! But her new husband is a dealer on the Riviera, and he has an uncle who possesses—or who might possess—the Gramercy jewels. That's who I'm going to see. I'm prepared to take a lot of chances to make sure."

"Good! But John, I must see you first. I'll come round——"

"I haven't ten minutes to squeeze in," Mannering said. "I've got to make emergency arrangements about French currency, tidy a lot of things up and be generally at pressure."

"But I must talk to you about this! The very thought that there might be a chance——"

"Why don't you behave more like a solicitor?" Mannering chided. "Be dispassionate, unemotional!"

Britten said abruptly: "Damn it, you ought to know why."

"That's a much better tone of voice," Mannering said. "I don't want Hilda or Tony to know, of course, but I'm telling you because I might get myself into a jam with the French police. If I do, tell Bristow what I've done and why, will you?"

"Yes. John, you know you don't have to take risks——" Britten's voice trailed off.

"Of course not," Mannering said dryly. "What is one more silken rope to me? I'd rather like that Bennett baby to have a father when it grows up, too. Not a word to anyone, but be ready for emergencies. I'll telephone or wire you as soon as I've settled a hotel at Chalon.'

"Try the Mirage," Britten said. "There'll be room at this time of the year. If I don't hear from you, I'll assume that's where you are."

"All right, the Mirage," Mannering agreed. "There's another thing. I don't know anything about French law, but I may want French legal aid. Do you know anything about it?"

"I've some clients with property on the Riviera, and I'm often dealing with lawyers in Nice and Cannes and along the coast," said Britten. "I'll put you right. Wouldn't it be a good idea if I were to come over, too?"

"Not yet," Mannering said.

"I could easily drop things here for a few days."

"Maybe later."

"Oh, all right," Britten said.

Mannering rang off, then called his bank and was told that it was impossible to get a business allowance of francs at such short notice. The manager also promised to try to do the impossible.

Meanwhile Larraby, Mannering's cherub-like manager, had obtained tickets for the afternoon plane to Nice. With Larraby and Carmichael, Mannering went into work for the next week; discussed sales which had to be visited, offers which should be made. But he was clear by the time Lorna arrived, with their bags packed, in time to get to London airport.

The weather was perfect. The flight was so calm that there was hardly a quiver. The channel was a blue mirror. They crossed the deep heart of rural France, and after four hours, were within sight of the Mediterranean. In a little over four, they landed at Nice. It didn't take them long to find a Renault taxi with a fierce-looking driver.

He appeared to take the hairpin bends in the beautiful corniche road to Chalon as a personal insult. He wrenched the wheel round, kept a finger on his horn, and tore along at fifty miles an hour when half the speed would have been too fast.

Lorna clutched Mannering's arm.

They caught glimpses of beauty. Below them, the blue of the Mediterranean, clear in the late evening air, the beach fringed with gay umbrellas, the white villas built into the hillside: but there were only glimpses. The stone wall, built to prevent the rock and rubble from falling across the road, was colourful with geraniums and bougainvillia, bright in the evening sun.

There was little traffic.

The driver turned a corner, and for a moment slowed down to show them the full magnificence of the sweeping bay, the white fringe against the beach, the hotels, the stately palms. Then he swooped downwards, as if he couldn't reach the promenade fast enough. When he reached it, there seemed no way in which he could avoid driving into the sea.

Instead, he pulled up outside a large hotel with a magnificent terrace. It was the Hôtel Mirage.

"M'sieu," he declared, "zis is ze best 'otel in all of France!"

A porter and two waiters were at the imposing entrance, looking as if they were anxious to vindicate the taxi driver's claim. The Mannerings went in, and two boys and an old porter took their luggage from the boot of the taxi. Soon, they had a fourth floor room at the front corner of the hotel. A balcony overlooked the bay on one side, and on the other, the headland which they had just driven down. From here, it looked peaceful.

Tips were distributed, everything signed and settled; and Lorna and Mannering stepped on to the balcony and looked towards the headland.

"I wonder which is Chalon's villa," Lorna said, without enthusiasm.

"It's that large white one high up on the headland— Stella pointed it out to me when I was over here before. It's floodlit at night."

"You haven't any second thoughts, or anything like that?" Lorna asked.

Mannering said with forced lightness; "Not yet, my sweet, but you never know."

He knew what was in her mind, knew that she almost certainly repented her mood of the night before. She would soon be asking herself why he should take wild and dangerous steps for people whom he knew only slightly. If she had asked him, he could not have answered or explained the driving force which compelled him.

"John," Lorna said, after a pause.

"Hm-hm?"

"You could have found out a lot about the villa if you'd asked Stella Dale."

"And told her that I was coming here."

"She'll guess, anyway."

"She won't have the faintest idea that I propose to burgle the place," Mannering said calmly. "Her husband is due to join her in London to-night, remember, and with the Count they're planning to stay there for two or three days. There are only servants and Raoul's brother Philippe at the house. I wouldn't rate it the biggest risk I've taken."

"You've no idea where they keep the jewels, what precautions they take, whether there's a strong-room."

"I'm going to find out," Mannering said, and kissed her lightly. "Stop worrying, my sweet."

It was like telling her to stop breathing.

The headwaiter, subtly prompted, was eager to talk about the Comte de Chalon. There was no better position near Chalon than M. le Comte's villa. After all, it was at the highest spot of the corniche. One reached the spot where all the coaches and sightseers stopped, and close by was the private road leading to the villa. He was a wonderful man.

The poor of Chalon, of Nice, of the whole coast and for many miles inland had cause to bless the name of M. le Comte. He was very rich and so generous—a prince of generosity. Thousands owed their lives to him, men, women and children. He was their saint.

Mannering became very thoughtful.

Dinner was superb. . . .

At half-past nine, a smart young man brought a smart new Renault to the door. Mannering signed a hire agreement, and the hotel was pleased to guarantee him, for he was not unknown on the Riviera.

He drove into Nice, and stopped some distance from a garage, then sent Lorna to buy the cheapest small car there; she drove away with an old Citroen, and followed Mannering to a spot on the promenade, away from the big hotels.

"We can park the little car here," Mannering said. "We'll find it useful."

"It cost most of our money."

"We'll be all right," Mannering said.

They drove up to the corniche in the Renault. It was a wide, smooth road which climbed higher and higher and spread before them first the fairyland of Chalon and, further away, of Nice and Cannes. Lights appeared to dance on the water and dangle from the sky.

Few other cars passed.

They reached a spot where the road was very wide, and saw a notice-board with a sign in English and in French. *Viewpoint.* They drew close to the wall, switched off the lights, and stepped out.

Below them, the headland fell sheer to the sea.

Above them, not far away, were the floodlights of the Villa Chalon. Within fifty yards of them were the gates leading to the house, with a light on top of one of the posts.

"Quite a spot," Mannering said.

"What are you going to do now?"

"Let's take a walk," said Mannering. He slid his arm under hers. "Just to make sure that we can find our way about if we ever get into a jam."

No one appeared when they walked towards the Villa Chalon, Mannering making mental notes of the twists in the drive, and hiding places near the house itself. He was not greatly worried by the floodlighting: that would almost certainly be switched off before long.

They walked back.

There was a gap in the protecting wall, not far from

the viewpoint, and a ledge just large enough to park the Renault. That would be useful, later.

"I can get down from the house and into the car in five minutes," Mannering said. "And back at the hotel before you realize I've been out at all."

"Don't you believe it," Lorna said. "I'm coming with you. I'll be waiting in the car."

"Don't expect to surprise me," Mannering said, and tucked her arm under his. "There shouldn't be much to worry about. You can wait for me, my sweet!"

As they drove back to the town, Lorna knew that he was beginning to feel that kind of excitement which had driven the Baron into such wild adventure. The fierce thrill would not subside until he had faced and overcome the challenge of the Villa. The desire to rescue Tony Bennett was not the only compelling factor now.

They left the hotel again at half-past twelve, took the Renault from its parking spot in a side street, and drove through a silent night.

6

THE VILLA

THE floodlights were off. There were no lights on the headland, few down in the bay.

The Mannerings had passed no one on the road.

They stood by the side of the Renault, in the darkness which was relieved only by a powdering of light from the stars. No one approached. They had been here for half an hour, and if anyone had seen them stop, inquiries would have been made by now.

A car approached, as they moved towards the gap in the wall through which Mannering had driven the car. Headlights blazed. They shrank back, until the car hummed past; the darkness seemed greater after that.

"How long shall I give you?" Lorna asked.

"Two hours or so," he said. "I'll flash a torch to you from the front door every thirty minutes. Give me five minutes grace!"

"All right," she said. He felt the tight clutch of her fingers. "Don't—don't ask for trouble."

Mannering caught her close, kissed her fiercely, and then moved swiftly away. The darkness swallowed him, and his voice came out of it. "I'll be back."

He reached the gates, walked up the drive, taking short cuts here and there over stony ground, sure that what stones he dislodged would not be noticed.

When he reached the lawns which surrounded the villa, he stood still. His heart was beating fast, and it wasn't from exertion. He waited until it steadied, then walked towards the back of the house. There, the windows and doors were hidden by trees and rocks, and there was little chance of the torchlight being seen. Anyone on the road would notice a light at the front.

He reached the back door.

He opened his coat and rubbed the palms of his hands together. Like those of the thief who had murdered Bernard Dale, the tops of his fingers were covered with adhesive plaster. It was a warm night, and his palms felt greasy. The tool-kit, fashioned as a waistband round his waist, seemed very hot at the small of his back.

He dried his hands on a piece of towelling, put that back in his pocket, and turned to the door. He shone a pocket torch on to it, examined the lock, decided that it would not be easy to force. He looked at the windows, going very close, and shining the torch against the side. His breathing was hushed.

He saw a cable close to the window, inside.

"It's wired for alarm," he murmured to himself. "I suppose that was inevitable."

But it hadn't been; and it would slow him down. With the windows and doors wired to raise an alarm once entry was forced, even more caution was necessary. Mannering formed his lips into a soundless whistle as he backed away.

Would the first-floor windows be wired?

There was a spot where he could climb up to one; and he climbed swiftly, making little noise. Pressing against the window, he shone the torch and saw the now familiar electric cable.

The Count de Chalon being a collector, it wasn't surprising that he took precautions against burglary. But these were extreme precautions.

Mannering still whistled, silently.

He climbed down, and went round to the front, shone his torch for a moment, and saw an answering flash from Lorna's. He went to a side window, and set to work.

In the days of the Baron all of this had been familiar;
there was no real strangeness now. He damped thick,
gummed brown paper with a sponge from a small rubber
bag, pressed it close to a pane of glass, and when it was
stuck, rapped at the glass sharply. There was a dull thud
as it broke. He tapped half a dozen times, then pulled the
paper away; pieces of glass stuck to it.

Old-fashioned methods were often best.

He pulled the splinters of glass from the side of the
window frame and then shone the torch inside. The
alarm wire stretched across the bottom of the window.
How delicate was it? Some would start the wailing alarm
the moment they were touched; others would stand a lot of
pressure before the alarm was raised.

He studied this closely, his head inside the house, his
shoulders outside. It looked new; and if it were new it
was probably very sensitive.

He studied the window again.

The small wooden frames were about eight inches by
ten. With four of them out, he would probably be able to
squeeze through without touching the alarm wire at all;
but it would take a lot of time.

He took a small saw from the kit, pressed it into a
rubber handle, and began to work. The noise of the saw
sounded very loud.

He stopped; the silence was complete. He waited
several minutes, heard nothing, and started again.

He sawed through one strut of the frame.

Now that he had started, the work was almost mono-
tonous; and it seemed to take longer than it need.

Twenty minutes' work made a hole large enough to
climb through. He stopped, and rested against the wall.
He was sweating freely, and there seemed to be no air, no
breath of wind from the sea. He strolled round to the
front of the house and flashed the torch again. Lorna's

came at once; a sign that she was on edge, looking this way all the time.

He put his tools back in the waistband, then began to climb through the hole in the window, putting his right leg in first, finding the floor on the other side, then crouching until he could get his head and shoulders through.

Soon, he stood upright in the room.

He shone the torch, found the door and went across.

Beyond was a passage; beyond that, the spacious hall and the front door. It was locked and bolted, and the alarm wire stretched tightly across. He needed to find the electric main switch, and walked along several passages until he found the kitchen.

The meters and switches were in a cupboard in the big, tiled room. The light from his torch reflected eerily from the shiny white tiles and the chromium taps.

He found the main switch and pressed it up, then went to the door and pressed down an ordinary light switch. Nothing happened. To make quite sure that all was safe, he pulled the alarm wire across the back door. There was no sound. He pushed back the bolts and unlocked the door, leaving it latched; that was a way of escape open. He went to the front door and shone the torch three times. Lorna would not expect another signal for a while after that.

Then he began to prowl. . . .

Until then, he had been thinking only of the immediate task; forcing entry, cutting off the current, sending word to Lorna, finding his way about the house. Now that was over, more urgent questions thrust at him. Where would the Count de Chalon keep his jewels? Hiding places, safes and strong-rooms were usually in the same kind of position in different houses; find the study, find the safe. But Chalon was a collector with a valuable collection somewhere here. He would probably have a strong-room.

The villa was built against the rock; rock had been hewn out for its foundations. The best place for a strong-room, obviously, was deep inside the rock. He need waste no time looking in those rooms with outside walls.

He found a book-lined room on the ground floor, judged from the position of the windows that it overlooked the bay; and from the position of the opposite wall, that it was built close against the rock. He opened a window and looked out, to make sure. There was the face of the rock, quite close.

Mannering went to the wall which backed on the rock, used the torch and studied the books and the shelves, running his hand up and down, seeking a catch which might make shelves swing open.

He found nothing.

He stood back, studying the books which showed up clearly where the torch struck them, and faded away at the sides, then he went forward and knelt down. He pulled back the carpet, which was flush with the bottom of the book-cases. There were polished boards beneath, and in one of them a recess had been carved; in the middle of the recess was a tiny plastic button.

He took a thin, asbestos glove from his pocket, put it on his right hand, and pressed the button. There might be an independent supply of electricity which he hadn't yet found.

He heard a click, then a sliding sound. He glanced up and saw part of the bookshelves opening. He moved back, waiting until all movement stopped. His heart was beating very fast.

There was a dark cavity beyond the bookcases.

Mannering stepped forward, with the torch beam shining on an iron door.

Needing more light, he took a larger torch from the kit,

and shone it on the door. It was built into the rock, and
looked to be steel. There was no keyhole, but a round
steel handle jutted out. If this were electrically controlled,
he would need the power on again.

He pulled; and nothing happened.

With the brighter light, he examined the door and the
rock wall which surrounded it. He found a switch inside
the rock where it had been hollowed out, and pressed;
nothing happened. He turned away, hurried back to the
kitchen, and switched the current on at the main again.
Within two minutes he was back at the steel door. He
used the asbestos glove, taking no chances, and pressed
the switch.

He heard a click, followed by a momentary humming
sound; that stopped.

He gripped the handle and pulled—and the door began
to open. He stood to one side, watching tensely, his heart
pounding. The door was open wide enough for him to
squeeze through; he made no move, just stood behind
the door and continued pulling.

He heard a sneeze of sound; another; and fast upon
each, a thud, as of a bullet going into the wall opposite.
He still pulled at the door.

Nothing else happened.

When it was wide open, he stepped in front of it, and
shone the torch against another door—a door of steel
bars this time. Fastened to it, carefully balanced on a
spring so that it would fire when the door was opened, was
an automatic pistol. The muzzle pointed at Mannering's
stomach. He did not need more telling that those two
thuds had been from bullets; or that the Count de Chalon
took remarkable steps to make sure that he wasn't
burgled.

He went to the front door, disconnected the alarm wire,
opened the door cautiously, and shone the torch.

Lorna's flashed back at him.

He went back, fighting against the temptation to hurry. There was still the barred door. He reached it and examined it cautiously, found the switch and pressed. He pushed the door open cautiously; there were no more surprises. He stepped forward into the strong-room, and for the first time, pressed down a light switch.

Light flooded the room.

This was large—long and narrow, and much more spacious than any room in the Chelsea flat. There were three safes, and a number of crates; and, hanging from wires stretched across the ceiling, a dozen paintings. One glimpse told Mannering that the pictures were worth a fortune. He was near one—and caught his breath in surprise. It was a Corot, stolen some months ago.

He recognized a dozen different paintings and *objets d'art*, some large and difficult to move freely—and all were stolen. The Count, perhaps with the knowledge of his nephews, was a collector of stolen goods; and hoarded them as a miser hoarded gold.

Mannering went to the nearest safe.

His heart was thumping with tension and anxiety. There was no time to force the locks of three safes, if each was as modern as the strong-room. He might have succeeded thus far, and still fail.

The tension reached a screaming point in his mind.

Slowly, he relaxed.

He could open the safes; compared with the strong-room door, they were old. The Baron had opened many like them, and saw no difficulty—needed just a little time. He took out the tools he needed, knelt down, and began.

He could think more freely now.

He had been in the villa more than an hour and a half. It was half-past two. He must be away from here by five at the latest. He wished that Lorna had not waited with the car. He kept picturing her face, and imagining her brushing her hair as she had on the morning when he had heard of Bernard Dale's death.

He could picture Dale's face, too; the ready smile and the warm nature of the man. He remembered how desperately Dale had been hurt when Stella had left him.

He saw Tony Bennett, staring incredulously at the judge's black cap.

He could think of those things while he worked.

In ten minutes, he felt the lock clock open. He stood to one side as he pulled, wary of yet another trick; but there was none.

Inside the safe were jewel cases.

He took several out, carried them to a wooden crate, opened them and began the search. There were jewels here he had neither seen nor heard of; beautiful gems. He felt their almost magnetic attraction; he wanted to study them, examine all their beauty. That was always a danger—that the brightness and the beauty of diamonds, above all others, would fascinate, almost hypnotize him, and destroy his judgment.

He went through case after case, and did not see the Gramercy stones.

There were three cases still unopened. He did not trouble to take these to the crate, but opened the first where he knelt; and the first diamonds which scintillated up at him were the Gramercys. He hadn't a moment's doubt.

7

SHOCK

Mannering peered down at the diamonds.

Their beauty made his breath come in short, sharp gasps. He had felt like that when he had first seen these small but exquisite stones. He could remember holding them in the calipers, while Bernard Dale had studied each one closely. Dale had felt the same about all good diamonds; they could take possession of him.

Mannering forced himself to close the case, and to open the next. These were the emeralds and the sapphires together; in the third case were the rubies. So this part of the chase was over.

He felt a sense of anti-climax.

His forehead was wet, and he drew his sleeve across it. Yet the strong-room was cool. There were a dozen jewel cases over there on the crates; and if some stolen jewels were here, the others might be stolen too.

He looked round the spacious strong-room, with the bright light shining mercilessly in every corner. There was a dark brown leather valise. He went across and picked it up, finding it empty. He went back to the crate and put all the jewels into the valise; there was plenty of room after all were inside.

He looked at the other safes.

This was always the temptation—always the danger. Here was a fortune, ready for the taking, but the other safes seemed to beckon him to stay.

He felt the sweat beading his forehead again.

"Don't be a *fool*," he breathed.

He picked up the valise and stepped towards the door. The jewels were heavy. He stopped in the big room, with the bookcase entrance to the strong-room open. He put the valise down, pressed the switch, and watched the doors close one after the other. Then he pushed the bookcases flush with the wall. Only the bullet holes were left to show that there had been a burglary. They were deep in wood panelling beneath a picture, and would only be noticed if someone looked at that section of the wall.

He went to the desk, forced the middle drawer open, took out a cash box and stuffed the contents in his pocket, then hurried into the dining-room, which was across the passage. He pushed several pieces of silver into the valise, and hurried along the hall towards the front door. When the burglary was first discovered, the stolen trifles might be thought to be the thief's only loot. Resident servants might not know how to get into the strong-room.

He felt fear creeping into him—that at the last moment he would run into trouble.

There was no sound.

He disconnected the alarm, opened the front door and stepped on to the porch. Welcome darkness met him. The night air stung his forehead and his lips. He closed the door very softly; there was hardly a sound.

He put the valise down and flashed the torch.

"I'm on my way," he said *sotto voce*.

He waited for the responding flash; none came.

He flicked his torch on again, and waited, his breath coming more sharply. Only darkness lay below him, there was no flash of light.

He picked up the valise and walked towards the head of the drive. His footsteps made a slight sound, but there was none other, and no light behind him. He flashed the torch again, without response.

It was warm; and he felt coldness gripping him.

He turned and looked at the house, with its ghostly whiteness vague and eerie in the starlight. He felt a strange heaviness within him, as if this were a house of ill-omen. He went further along the drive, and the case seemed too heavy to carry far.

Every now and again he stopped, listening intently.

Lorna must have come up to meet him. She hadn't been able to stand the strain. Now rocks hid the torch from her. What other explanation could there be?

Mannering shone the torch again, but no longer really expected to see the responding light.

It didn't come.

There was no sound, and had Lorna been coming up the drive or even scrambling across the grounds, he would have heard her.

The road and the drive gates were only thirty yards away.

Car headlights appeared a long way off, brightening the gloom with a misty brilliance. The light grew brighter and Mannering could hear the beat of the engine. Soon the light carved through the darkness near the drive gates and by the wall which protected the road from the sheer fall to the rocks and the bay. Great, dark shadows formed; but there was no sign of Lorna.

The car swept past, and darkness followed it.

Mannering reached the road, and then began to run towards the gap in the wall, and the Renault. He had to fight against the urge to shout. Her name was on his lips and he forced it back.

He reached the gap.

The car was there.

"Lorna!" he called.

There was no answer.

He took the torch from his pocket and swept the light round. It was reflected from the shiny paintwork and the windows. He peered inside, but Lorna wasn't there. The despairing hope that she might have sat inside and fallen asleep, died in him.

"*Lorna!*"

From far below there was the rustle of the sea. Apart from that, the only sound was his own breathing.

He turned and looked towards the villa, but there was no light; no light anywhere. The whole night was dark and had swallowed her up.

"*Lorna, Lorna, Lorna!*"

The name echoed back at him, mockingly.

"This—won't—do," he said. His voice wasn't steady but at least he didn't shout. The silent darkness put ill-formed fears into his mind. He dared hardly think. He went towards the wall, peering downwards; the stars reflected on the dark bosom of the water. He remembered the drive from the airfield, and the sharp, angry rocks below at this point in the corniche.

Had Lorna walked, slipped, and fallen? What else *could* have happened?

Had she walked, slipped, fallen?

He knew that the fall on to the hungry rocks was sheer in places; that she might have fallen and been killed instantaneously; or that she might be lying down there now, her body broken but conscious, and in pain. The demons tore at his nerves.

There had been hours of tension at the villa, hours of a physical and mental strain; now that he needed to relax he could not—there was that dark dread.

"*Lorna! Lorna!*"

Only the echo and the whispering sea came back to him.

He moved again, and was surprised at the difficulty of movement; it was as if his muscles and his joints were locked. He shone his torch and saw other tyre-tracks—but there was more. He could see the gravel, scuffed up as it would be if there had been a struggle. He reached the car again and opened the door with clumsy fingers, put the valise inside, slammed the door, and then got into the driving seat. He felt quite sure that there had been a struggle before Lorna had been overpowered. He switched on the headlights. They were yellow and dim; disappointing. The other cars had had brighter lights; they were English, these were French.

He saw a shadowy movement.

He started the engine, as if he had noticed nothing. The shadow appeared again—he thought it was of a man, crouching by the wall.

He jammed on the brakes, suddenly.

There was a man, who jumped up and became clear in the headlamps; he carried a gun. His face was masked, but his eyes glittered.

"You! Put up your hands!" He spoke softly, clearly, as Mannering opened the door.

The man came close.

Mannering stepped out, alarm for Lorna tormenting him. The man was very close. Mannering raised his hands, slowly, as if meaning to obey; and then jumped. The risk was between life and death.

The gun went off, with a roar, the flash was vivid—but Mannering crashed into the man, feeling no hurt. He caught the other's wrist, and twisted; after a moment's vicious struggling, the gun dropped. Mannering smashed at the masked face, but the other brought up his knee, and drove the wind out of his stomach. Mannering staggered back, but the light showed the other as well as the gun.

Mannering grabbed it.

The man turned and ran, and leapt over the wall out of the range of the headlamps.

Gasping for breath, Mannering turned back to the car as he heard the stutter of a motor-cycle.

He saw the machine moving down the road; its lights went out, and there was no sign of it, only the noise. Almost without thinking, he got into the car, started the engine, and moved off. At heart, he knew there was little hope of catching up with the motor-cyclist, but he had to try in desperate hope.

Facts forced themselves into his mind.

Lorna had been kidnapped; and a man had been waiting here, probably for the jewels. He didn't try to think beyond that as he drove, but he saw nothing, no sign of the motor-cycle.

He reached the Hôtel Mirage without seeing anyone else on the road; and he hadn't been followed.

But Lorna——

The night porter stood up from his chair by the steps.

"Any message for me?" Mannering asked abruptly. "For Mannering."

"Non, m'sieu, zere ees none." The porter looked at the valise.

Mannering said: "Take me up, quickly."

"Oui, m'sieu."

The porter was slow; it seemed an age before they reached the floor. Mannering strode towards his room, the porter following leisurely.

The room was empty.

"M'sieu," murmured the porter, and put the valise down.

There was no message; nothing.

Mannering made himself open the valise. He saw Lorna's face on the jewel cases; everywhere; but it wouldn't help Lorna if he ran into more trouble; and the jewels could damn him.

Where should he put them?

He looked about the room, tensely. There were a dozen

obvious hiding places, but he wanted one that was almost foolproof. There might be little time.

He stood on the bed and examined the centre light-fitting, of gilded metal, big, and hollow. He unfastened it from the ceiling, and lifted it down carefully. He took the metal parts to pieces, without trouble, and put jewels in wherever there was room. Most were in the large main stem which hung down from the ceiling.

He heard people stirring, outside.

One or two people walked in the hotel.

He worked feverishly, until the fitting was back in position, only a few small pieces of plaster and a light powdering of the plaster showed that anything had been disturbed.

The jewel-cases remained with the silver oddments.

He put all of these into a valise, then took it out. He had to get rid of them, quickly; the best place, for now, would be in the old Citroen car.

He slipped out of the bedroom without being seen, found an alcove and watched for five minutes.

No one appeared or approached his door. He wasn't followed.

It was warm outside, the first glow of daylight was in the sky and touching the sea. With Lorna, this would have been perfect.

He reached the Citroen, put the contents of the valise into the tiny boot, then drove the little car to a different parking place. He went back to the hotel, quite sure that he had not been followed.

But the room might have been searched.

He unlocked the door and stepped into the little hall. Darkness greeted him. He opened the bedroom door. The curtains were drawn, so the room was also in darkness.

Before the door closed, he called impulsively: "Lorna!"

There was a sound; as of someone stirring in bed.

No, no, this was impossible, she hadn't come back! If she had come back, she would have left a message somehow.

He took out the motor-cyclist's gun, then thrust the inner door open and switched on the light—stopped quite still.

A girl, not Lorna, lay on his bed.

She was young, and easy to look at. Her auburn hair, glinting under the light, was wavy and unruly. Her cheeks were flushed, and she had honey-coloured eyes and a dimple; she was impossibly country-maidish, had Mannering been in the mood to realize it. She wore a strapless dress, which revealed her lovely shoulders.

She blinked at him.

"No," said Mannering, in a taut voice. "I can't have come to the wrong room." He felt as if he were losing his wits, as he turned towards the door. He pulled open the other door, reached the passage, and stopped abruptly.

His key had opened the door.

He swung back into the bedroom. The girl was sitting up, and punching a big, square pillow behind her back. In spite of her youth, she had a figure that was little short of voluptuous, and her smile was lazily seductive. There was no doubt that she had been asleep. She yawned and stretched her arms, as if drawing his attention to her figure with feline cunning and grace.

"Hallo," she said. The word told him that she was French, the "H" hardly sounded at all, the "o" was uttered on a high, musical note.

"What——" Mannering gulped. Shock, anxiety, urgency, suspense and now this baggage, combined to bemuse him. He became earnest. "What the devil are you doing here?"

She smiled, delightfully.

"You *are* M. Mannering?"

"I——"

"If you are M. Mannering, I 'ave a message for you."

He wanted to grab her creamy shoulders and shake her until the truth was forced out; and she seemed to know that. Her tawny eyes, flecked with green, mocked him.

"I am—Mannering," he made himself say.

"That is good." She smiled again; her teeth were very white, her lipstick was as thick as if she were going out to the shops or the promenade. "I am Lucille Rivierè."

Mannering couldn't keep still any longer. He went forward, clutched at her shoulders, felt his fingers bury themselves deep in her warm flesh.

"Where is my wife?"

"Your wife is quite safe, m'sieu," said the girl who called herself Lucille, "she will remain so"—laughter and malice gleamed in her eyes—"if you do what you are told. Do you understand, m'sieu?"

8

THREAT

MANNERING's fingers were still imbedded deeply in the girl's shoulders. He leaned over her; their faces were very close together. He must be hurting, but she gave that lazy smile—insolence and mockery and malice were all combined.

"And the first thing I tell you to do is to release me," she said.

Mannering moved away, and stood at the side of the bed, looking down at her. The marks of his fingers showed. Two things warred in his mind; the desire to hurt, to make her tell the truth, to lead him to Lorna; and fear, that if he did the wrong thing he might not be able to help Lorna.

"Do not be so worried," the girl said lightly. "All will be 'appy for you. I think your wife is most charming."

"Have you—seen her?"

"Oh, yes," said Lucille. She sat upright and began to rub her shoulders gingerly, arms folded across her breasts in order to do so. "I was there when she was taken away."

Mannering moistened his lips.

"She was a little frightened but she was not hurt," said Lucille reassuringly. "I had to wait here to give you the message, and I was very tired. You do not mind me sleeping on your bed?" There was as much mischief as malice in her eyes. "Sit down, m'sieu. Perhaps you would like a drink."

"Who is working with you?" he asked abruptly.

"Oh, a friend. You saw him, I believe—on his motor-cycle." She beamed. "He was to take the jewels, but a gun did not frighten you, so—we try this way."

Mannering didn't sit down, but moved across to the wardrobe, opened it, took out a bottle of whisky and a glass, and poured a finger.

"That will make you feel better," Lucille approved. "I do not like it when there is such a wild look in your eyes. You are a most handsome man! Such courage, also. You impressed my friend."

Her eyes glistened.

"Lucille," said Mannering, and was glad, almost grateful, that he could keep his voice steady. "Get up."

"But it is so late, and the chair is quite comfortable for you."

He contemplated her for a few moments, then said:

"I'll be back." He moved across to the door.

"Stop! Where are you going?" Lucille asked quickly.

He didn't speak or look round at her, but made his way out of the room, locking the door behind him. He thought that she was alarmed; she hadn't expected him to leave. He went into the passage; he wanted to collect his thoughts, to fight back the temptation to shake the truth out of her.

The fact that she had mentioned the motor-cyclist almost certainly proved that she was the man's accomplice. She might be there to search the room; or simply as a messenger.

Just above the bed she lay on, were the jewels.

Steadier, he went back to the room.

The girl was standing by the window, a fur cape over her shoulders. All trace of tiredness had vanished. She smiled, but he thought that she was less confident than she had been when he had first arrived; and he was sure she was relieved to see him back.

"Don't do any more foolish things, m'sieu."

"Not now, not any time," Mannering said. "What do you want? Where's my wife?"

"What would I want but the jewels?" she asked. "You give me them, and your wife will be quite all right."

He could easily say the wrong thing and jump into trouble. He was doubly glad, now, that he had gone out to get a grip on himself.

"I don't know what jewels you're talking about. If I did, you wouldn't get one, my beauty, until my wife is back. Go and find your boy friend. Tell him my wife must be here by"—he looked at his watch; it was a little after five-thirty. "Nine o'clock sharp."

"M. Mannering——"

Now he could let himself go.

"Get to hell out of here and tell him!" Mannering took the girl's shoulders and bundled her out of the room. He heard her gasp for breath as she staggered away from the door, but he didn't wait to listen. He flung himself across the room and snatched up the telephone.

"Hall porter, please."

"A moment, m'sieu."

Mannering waited, feverishly impatient; then the porter answered, and Mannering spoke in fluent French.

"There is a young lady coming downstairs, in a brown dress and wearing a fur wrap."

"Yes, m'sieu."

"Stop her, talk to her, ask her what she is doing in the hotel," Mannering said. "Delay her for at least five minutes. It will be worth five thousand francs to you."

"*Merci*, m'sieu. And what shall I do *after* the five minutes?"

"Let her go."

"I understand," said the porter, almost as if he meant it. "Ah, she is here."

Mannering rang off.

He jumped across the room, opened a case, and took a small make-up case from it. He stood in front of the mirror, using greasepaint, working cheek-pads into his mouth, broadening his nostrils with plastic pieces. There was no time at all for fineness. He snatched a blue polo sweater from the case, slipped into it, ruffled his hair, and pulled on a blue beret. Then he hurried downstairs.

"Mam'selle, I am so sorry," the night porter was saying, "but I must know——"

The girl was hemmed in by his desk, looking frantically right and left. Mannering dodged back out of sight, and went to the nearest telephone.

In a moment, the hall porter said: " 'Allo?"

"Let her go in a few seconds," Mannering said.

He went out by a side door, and hurried across the road to the wide promenade. Several other people were there in the warmth of the brightening dawn.

Lucille came running out.

She hurried to the kerb, and flung her leg over a little green velocipede, dozens of which buzzed along every street by day. The engine stuttered as Mannering went quickly towards his Citroen. He was at the wheel when the girl was a few hundred yards ahead, going fast.

She turned away from the sea, into a side street. Mannering raced round the corner, in time to see her disappear round another. That was into the narrow main road, where trams already clattered along the rails which stood up like welts in the cobbled road.

There were several cars and four velocipedes. Mannering kept the girl in sight, until, a hundred yards ahead, she turned left. This was into a wide street of tall houses, mostly in need of paint.

The girl was disappearing into a court-yard approached through green gates. Mannering drove straight past, but caught the number of the house from the corner of his eye. It was 27, painted white on a black circle on the drab green wall.

At the end of the road, he saw the name—rue de l'Arbre; at at that end the sea shimmered peacefully and the sky was blue delight.

Mannering turned the corner, and stopped.

If he went into the house now, he would probably run into serious trouble. Until he had Lorna safe, he couldn't hand the Gramercys over to the police; they were his chief barter. He had to play this with agonizing care—although it was like playing with Tony Bennett's life as well as with Lorna.

If he watched the house, he would know if she were taken away. But he couldn't watch all the time.

The temptation to break in was almost overwhelming, but Mannering fought it back. He was too tired, might do the wrong thing simply through lack of sleep.

A few hours' rest would make a new man of him.

There was always the chance that the man who had sent Lucille would take Lorna to the Mirage, hoping for a direct exchange with the jewels. He was much more likely to visit Mannering in person.

Mannering kept arguing with himself. He knew where to find the girl, if not Lorna; and Lorna was safe while he had the jewels.

The wise thing was to go back to the Mirage, rest, and wait until nine o'clock and word from Lucille's boy-friend.

He made himself go back. . . .

He parked the little car some distance from the hotel, rubbed off the greasepaint, walked to the hotel, entered by a side-door, paid the porter the promised five thousand francs, and soon reached his room. He glanced up at the light-fitting; it hadn't been touched. Everything was as he had left it.

He kicked off his shoes and took off his coat, then lay

on the bed. The faint smell of an unfamiliar perfume
teased him. He could picture the girl when she had first
blinked up at him, pink and sleepy. Mocking—tantaliz-
ing—malicious?

He made himself breathe regularly and deeply. If he
could drop off even for half an hour, it would do him
a world of good. All his life he had taught himself to
sleep when he had a chance; a tired man was always at a
disadvantage.

And Lorna had insisted on being with him!

There was nothing but irony. He could fix the Comte
de Chalon easily, now; could find out the truth because
his hand was so strong against the Count—or would have
been, but for Lorna.

And the auburn-haired girl.

And her boy-friend.

Mannering felt his eyes getting heavier. He heard
sounds about the hotel and others in the street; cars,
horses, bicycles, motor-bicycles, then people talking.

He dozed.

When he woke, bright sunlight shone on to the curtains.
He lay quite still, but awake on the instant, fully alert.

Someone was tapping at the door.

He called: "Come in," but the tapping was repeated.
He got off the bed, reached the outer door, and hesitated.

He glanced up at the light-fitting.

The burglary at the villa had probably been discovered
by now; possibly the servants knew that the strong-room
had been raided. The Count de Chalon and his nephew in
London might already know.

The tapping came again.

He opened the door.

The girl who called herself Lucille stood there. She
wore a lemon-coloured dress without sleeves, and a tiny
lemon-coloured hat, little more than a patch on the back

of her glorious hair, which fell in a gleaming, waving mass to her shoulders. She was lovely and she was young.

She smiled, almost timidly.

"Hallo," she said. "You are still here."

"And waiting for you," Mannering said grimly. "Come in."

She led the way into the bedroom, glancing about her—as if desperately anxious to spot the hiding place. Mannering rasped his fingers over his stubble, went to the balcony and stepped out, looking over the sea and the faint haze which dulled its blue brilliance. Some people were already bathing and there was a constant flow of traffic. Over on the headland, the haze hid the white shapes of the villas.

He turned to face Lucille.

"Where is my wife?"

"She has written you a letter." Lucille opened a large, bright green handbag, and took out a sealed envelope. Mannering just managed to prevent himself from snatching it. The girl was laughing at him; the girl could easily make him feel a fool.

But she didn't know that he had followed her to 27, rue de l'Arbre.

Did she?

He glanced down at the written *John Mannering*. That was Lorna's clear, bold handwriting; no one in the world would be able to deceive him about that.

"Have you see her?"

"Not since last night."

"Who gave you this?"

Her eyes spilled over with merriment.

"My good friend, m'sieu!"

He put his head on one side, and looked at her, then opened the letter. It was to his eternal credit that he didn't rip it open.

Lorna hadn't wasted words.

Darling, I can't understand it. They shanghaied me
last night, but I wasn't hurt. The only man I've seen is
delightful. I *think* I'm in a villa but don't know where.
The man says that I shall hear from you soon.

Darling, I *am* perfectly all right. This isn't written
under dictation, with a man standing over me with a
whip.

He tells me you're back at the hotel.

Be careful,
Lorna.

P.S. I haven't the faintest idea what he wants me to
do. He had a telephone call from a girl—woman?—
named Lucille.

Mannering read the letter twice. The weight lifted. He
could look into Lucille's tawny eyes and feel almost free
from fear. He didn't look at her. He knew that she was
watching him carefully, anxious to judge his reactions. He
folded the letter, slipped it into his pocket, turned and
looked out to sea.

"Are you satisfied?" Lucille asked.

Mannering grinned. "Not yet!"

He moved swiftly, shot out a hand, pulled her hair
lightly, and then went into the bedroom. She hurried
after him; and he thought that she was alarmed, in case
he ran off. He stripped off his shirt, singlet and trousers,
and she stood with her back to the balcony, eyes rounded,
lips parted.

Wearing just his running short pants, Mannering went
into the bathroom.

"Lucille!" he called.

She appeared at the door.

"If you're not very careful," Mannering said, splashing

hot water into the handbasin, "you'll get yourself into a lot of trouble. What's the name of this boy-friend of yours?"

"Philippe," she said with nervous promptness.

"Philippe what?"

Raoul, Stella's husband, had a brother Philippe.

"I am not allowed to tell you."

"I could find ways of making you tell me."

"Could you?" asked the girl, and seemed to become more confident; her eyes had that gleam of mockery again. "Perhaps Philippe would then find a way of making your wife do things she does not want to do."

"The cat puts out her claws."

"What is that?"

"Never mind." Mannering began to lather his face, vigorously. He finished, then shaved; he had never been watched so closely while shaving in his life. He turned and shooed her out. Relief had excited him, he was almost light-hearted.

"I'm going to have a bath. Order my breakfast, please."

"Very well. Bacon and eggs?"

"Continental breakfast," Mannering said. "Coffee, not tea."

"For such a big man?" She laughed at him, and then closed the door.

He heard her go straight into the bedroom, then heard the ting of the telephone. After that, he fancied that he heard her moving about.

He finished his bath, opened the door and called:

"Go and wait on the balcony, I'm coming out to dress."

She didn't answer. He waited for a minute or so, and went into the bedroom. He stopped abruptly, just inside.

Lucille wasn't there. A man stood with his back to the balcony, smiling.

9

SUGGESTION

THE man was young—in the early thirties, Mannering guessed. He was good-looking, dark-haired, rather swarthy skinned. His teeth looked very white when he smiled, and his dark eyes held a gleam which reminded Mannering of the look in Lucille's. Lean and tall, the man held himself well, was confident and capable.

"Good morning, Mr. Mannering."

Mannering said: "Who rubbed the lamp?"

The other frowned, puzzled.

"I beg your pardon?"

"Perhaps you don't have the story in France," said Mannering. He moved to the side of the bed, where his clothes were laid out. That startled him for a moment; he hadn't laid them out there. "Aladdin had a lamp. When he rubbed it he could work miracles. Such as change a girl into a fine, strikingly handsome chap like you." He pulled on the singlet. "Would you mind passing me the cigarettes on the dressing-table?"

"I shall be delighted." The man turned his back on Mannering, he had plenty of nerve. "Lucille has gone downstairs." He handed Mannering the cigarettes and struck a match.

"Thanks. Won't you smoke?"

"Never, until after *déjeuner*," said the man firmly.

"Wise man." Mannering went on dressing. He had finished when there was a tap at the door. He went to open it, and a waiter appeared, carrying a tray.

"Break*fass*, m'sieu!"

"Yes, thanks." Mannering stood aside.

The waiter bowed to the other man, pulled up a table and put the tray on it, then placed a chair so that Mannering could eat while looking out over the bay.

Mannering sat down and hitched up the chair.

The man watched him, expecting violence or the threat of violence, puzzled because neither came. The more puzzled, the better. Mannering was liberal with the butter and marmalade. He watched a little yacht far out in the bay, its sail very white; so out there the sun was breaking through the haze.

Finished, Mannering lit a cigarette and rested his elbows on the table, looked steadily into the other's dark eyes.

Tension grew.

Then Mannering said: "It's a lovely morning, isn't it?"

The other relaxed, smiled easily, and moved towards the bed. He sat on the side of it.

"I think we shall work well together, Mr. Mannering. Your wife is well, if puzzled."

"So her letter said."

"You conceal the fact that you are also puzzled very well indeed, Mr. Mannering."

Mannering murmured: "What's puzzling me?"

Philippe said: "I see!" His eyes glinted with laughter. In many ways he reminded Mannering of the girl. He had the same freshness, the same engaging manner; they were both likeable people it could be a joy to know. "Perhaps you are wondering where you were last night."

Mannering said blandly: "Oh, I think I know that."

"It was kind of you to visit M. le Comte in his absence."

"Really?"

"But he will be most distressed because of the burglary."

"Will he?"

"Very distressed," said Philippe. He moved towards

the head of the bed, and put his legs up. "If he realized that he had lost many of his jewels I think he would probably go mad, m'sieu. That would be a great shame, wouldn't it?"

"Perhaps you exaggerate," Mannering said.

"Oh, no, I don't think so," said Philippe. "After you had left, I also went there. It was easy for me to climb through the hole you made. I did not find it difficult to discover that you had been to the strong-room. I saw the bullets in the wall. It was easy for me, of course, because I knew where the strong-room was, although I would never have been able to force it open. I salute a *very* brilliant burglar."

"Not I," said Mannering firmly.

"My friend, it is useless to——"

"From the beginning I had a feeling that you were making a mistake," Mannering said regretfully. "Such things do happen. Shall we——"

"Somewhere you have concealed the Gramercy jewels," Philippe said. "Lucille and I were watching you. We followed you earlier in the evening, when you and your wife went to explore the headland. We watched, and saw you go to the villa alone.

"We saw you flash the signal to your wife, and saw her reply to it," he went on. "Shall we agree that there is no point in denying that you robbed M. le Comte?"

Mannering stubbed out his cigarette.

"We shall never agree," he said sadly.

Philippe said slowly, thoughtfully: "I wish I could understand what is making you behave like this, m'sieu. However, perhaps you will be more easily persuaded later. You are the famous John Mannering, of Quinns, in London. You have a business which extends throughout the world. You are a most reputable dealer in precious stones." Philippe's smile was almost feline, now. "And I

am sure that you have a most kind and generous heart.
Have you not, M. Mannering?"

Mannering didn't answer.

"I imagine that is certain, or you would not have come
here," said the other, gently. "You came, I understand—
may I say that I and my friends have reasoned out your
motives?—to find the Gramercy jewels. You hoped that
might help a young man now in grave danger of hanging.
That is very sad, m'sieu. I wish that I could help."

Still Mannering kept silent.

"But I cannot," said the other, with a shrug. "It is
sad—but it is fate. M. Mannering, here in France there
are many poor people who have great difficulty in keeping
themselves alive. Even their children are underfed. It is a
great country but it has so much sadness, much poverty.
And nearby, in Spain and Italy, many people are even
worse off—far worse off than your friend in London,
perhaps. Troubles are comparative, you will agree?"

Mannering said: "Yes," and wondered how long it
would be before he knew what the other was driving at.

"We reach agreement at last," beamed the Frenchman.
"I hope it is the first of many! M'sieu, you have been to
the Villa Chalon. You found stolen goods and jewels
there." He shrugged his shoulders. "Also, you have taken
great personal risk by forcing your way in. The law is
very severe in France, m'sieu. And there is the little
matter of your wife's comfort and happiness to
remember."

His smile flashed, his teeth gleamed.

Mannering said very softly: "Yes, we agree about that,
too. Don't go too far, I can get vicious."

"But my friend, *I* have the gun! You know," went on
the Frenchman, changing his tone and becoming almost
conspiratorial, "I can see much in you that is in me. You
snap your fingers at the law—they are fools, you say. I

shall break into a house to prove them wrong. A very fine attitude. Who is to blame you for choosing the wrong house at the wrong time? But let me return to your natural generosity, m'sieu. Those people who are in need, the hungry and the sick who get no help from la belle France—do they deserve their misery, m'sieu?"

Mannering didn't speak.

"Somehow I do not think you would condemn them, like so many others, as hopeless fools, the cattle or the fodder for clever men like you and me. They need help, M. Mannering. I can tell you something about that. My good uncle, M. le Comte de Chalon, is a great collector of precious stones. He is also a great benefactor to the poor."

"Indeed," Mannering said heavily.

"I will tell you something more. In this part of the world, this beautiful coast line, there are thousands of fat pigs guzzling their expensive food, gloating over their jewels, squandering their money at Monte Carlo and the other casinos. All that is true, m'sieu. They come from all parts of the world, as well as from France. But there are millions in need. My uncle helps these. If he sometimes has jewels which do not belong to him——" Philippe shrugged. "Is it so great a crime? He needs them to sell for the poor, m'sieu."

Mannering didn't speak.

"And for his good work he wants all the jewels you stole. In return for them, you shall have your wife back. To make sure you do not go to the police, we point out that we can prove you robbed the villa—and you will be able to prove nothing. The jewels, m'sieu. I want them, now."

"When my wife——" began Mannering, and stopped.

Philippe stood quite still, his eyes very bright, there was a different tone in his voice. Something in him changed, too; for the first time Mannering was able to believe that this man could be deadly. The pleasantness, the flippancy and the courtesy were all part of him, but underneath there was a different man—a dangerous man.

"I make the terms, Mannering. Remember this: You sold the Gramercy jewels to Dale," he said, "and cleared the cheque at once. Early next morning an expert safe-breaker stole those jewels from Dale, and killed Dale. Suppose I tell the police that you came to me yesterday and offered to sell me the Gramercy and other doubtful jewels, but I refused because I recognized them as stolen property."

"No one would believe you," said Mannering, but his heart was thumping.

"No? Where were you on the night of the murder?"

"At home with my wife."

"Not a good alibi, m'sieu. And when you are found with the stolen jewels in your possession, and the Gramercys—I don't know what you've done with them, but they can't be far away—are traced to you . . ."

Mannering took out cigarettes, lit one, and let the smoke drift towards the balcony. He said softly:

"Has it ever occurred to you, Philippe, how easy it would be for me to break your neck?"

Philippe said sharply: "We will be serious."

"I'm quite serious. Dale was murdered for the Gramercys. I'm going to get his murderer."

"He is about to die, he has been tried, found guilty, and——"

"A little mistake," Mannering said softly. "You've made one, too——" He moved suddenly, swiftly, and Philippe backed away, but didn't shoot. Mannering had an odd conviction that he did not mean to use the gun. Mannering pushed it aside, and cracked a blow on the Frenchman's chin. Philippe fell backwards against the wall—holding the gun, not shooting.

"My wife," said Mannering, "where is she?"

Philippe stood up, rubbing his jaw. His eyes were cold. "You go too far, Mannering."

"If my wife isn't returned, quickly, I shall go to the police, and——"

"I do not think you will," Philippe said. "Your wife has not been hurt—*yet*. She will remain as our guest hostage to your good behaviour." He glanced down at the pistol, then slipped it back into his pocket. "We are nice people, Mannering, and we enjoy life, but—we can be cruel. Sometimes it is necessary to be cruel. We should not wish to hurt your wife. We simply want the jewels back, and a way of ensuring your silence. Shall we give ourselves a little time to think?"

He smiled; and his teeth were brilliant white against his swarthy skin.

He turned round slowly, opened the door, and went out.

10

LUCILLE

MANNERING stepped out on to the balcony.

He looked down at the terrace, which was almost deserted; but Lucille sat at a table not far from the orchestra platform. The sun caught her yellow dress and the absurd little hat, and turned her hair to gleaming brilliance. She was sipping an aperitif. A waiter stood near, looking at her, as if her charms affected him.

She looked up, then stood up.

Philippe appeared. Mannering could not see his face, but saw his gesture. The girl smiled. They both sat down, and the waiter approached, then went off quickly. Philippe leaned forward; his dark head hid Lucille's face but not her glorious hair.

The waiter came up again, with a glass.

Lucille looked grave.

Mannering turned and went into the bedroom. It seemed desolate. He lit another cigarette, frowning. Emotions warred in him; fresh fears for Lorna, anxiety for Tony, who was within a few days of the gallows. Up there in the light-fitting were the Gramercys; if he gave them to the police, told them where he had found them——

He was losing his wit. No one would believe him; he had to find proof that Tony wasn't the murderer. Possession of the jewels, and the knowledge that they'd been at the Villa Chalon, would help. But with Lorna in danger, he was hamstrung.

There was the house in rue de l'Arbre—but he would

have to go there after dark. At least Philippe could not suspect that he knew the house.

Could he?

Was Lorna still there?

He ought to disguise himself and keep watch. He needed a helper badly.

He took out Lorna's letter and read it again.

She had not seen Philippe take out the gun; or seen his expression or heard his voice when he had said: "Sometimes it is necessary to be cruel. We should not like to hurt your wife."

Lorna knew only the smiling side.

There was another angle; did the police yet know anything?

The police of Chalon, Nice and Cannes—in fact along the whole length of the Riviera, might soon be hunting for a thief. Philippe and the others might not be able to keep the robbery secret.

Mannering felt suffocated.

He went out, thinking of Philippe. He might be Raoul Bidot's brother, but that wasn't certain. The only certainties were that the jewels had been at the villa, Philippe wanted them, and had kidnapped Lorna.

There was another certainty: he dare not go to the police, had to handle this by himself. He couldn't wait for darkness and a visit to 27, rue de l'Arbre.

He went out.

Half a dozen more people were on the terrace, now; and Lucille was alone at the table where he had seen her. He showed no sign that he recognized her, but walked out, and crossed to the promenade. The little Citroen was in sight, one of dozens of parked cars, now. The Renault was also in sight. He wanted to get the Citroen away as soon as he could, and dump the jewel cases and the silver.

A slight wind was rustling the fringes of the gay

umbrellas. The haze had gone. The headland showed up, vivid green, and the villas showed clearly, too; he picked out Villa Chalon.

He turned right, away from the town. A few people sat watching the sea, a few bathed, and children clambered about the pebbles. He didn't look behind, but thought that Lucille was following. After ten minutes, he made sure. She was thirty or forty yards behind.

He quickened his pace. The made-up promenade came to an end. Along here was hard sand, a few tufts of grass and a steep bank to the pebbly beach.

Mannering looked round again.

Lucille, still behind him, looked very hot. She waved. He climbed down to the beach, heard her coming, and saw her slide down the last few feet.

" 'Allo," she said, and was almost reproachful. "Must you walk so fast?"

"I wanted to make you tired."

"M'sieu," said Lucille, "you have succeeded!" She was flushed, breathing rather hard. She sank down grace-fully on the pebbles, legs bent beneath her, flared skirt making a canopy. "Please give me a cigarette."

He gave her one; lit up for them both.

"Thank you. If you are wise, M. Mannering, there will be no trouble for you or for your wife. She will have a very happy time. But—tell me where the jewels are."

Mannering didn't speak.

"You see, m'sieu," Lucille went on very earnestly, "there is little else you can do. Philippe *can* be cruel. We understand that it will take a little time for you to see the wisdom of taking our advice." She leaned back on her hands and blew smoke towards the sea; and he did not doubt that she knew quite well what a magnificent picture she made. "We shall not lose our patience, m'sieu. A day, two days—what difference will it make?"

"Tell Philippe I'll think about it—when my wife is back."

"But, m'sieu," went on Lucille, with even greater earnestness, "he will not send her back until he has the jewels. You can make it very difficult or very pleasant for your wife. It is up to you."

Mannering looked away.

After a long pause, Lucille went on:

"The differences in men are strange, John." She slurred the J attractively, using his Christian name with obvious intent. "Some are miserable without their wives, others"—he didn't look at her, but could imagine her shrug—"they are overjoyed! You are one of the miserable ones, I can see."

"Am I?" he asked mildly.

She laughed at him.

"Most certainly! But I am to make sure that you do not run away, John!" She leaned forward and took his hands. "Help me up, please."

He pulled her up. She leaned against him longer than was necessary. They walked along, feet crunching the pebbles.

Mannering helped her climb the bank to the promenade.

"Of course," she said, "I have others to help me watch you."

He glanced at two men who stood against the wall of a house, across the road. They didn't look this way. He had seen them outside the Hôtel Mirage, without really noticing them.

Lucille took his arm and they walked back towards the town. The two men followed.

"You see," said Lucille, "we are very thorough. Just tell me when you are ready to give us the jewels. I have a room at the hotel—next door to yours. It is all arranged and it is all very simple." They were walking very slowly; ambling. "You must not make mistakes, like trying to find out where your wife is or anything like that. Do you see what I mean?"

"I see," said Mannering.

It was not until he was alone in his room that he felt that he could breathe freely; not until then that the last of the chains were off his mind. The trap had been set so cleverly and the doors behind him seemed tightly closed. But his only trump was the jewels—and they could be used against him, if they were found.

The same thoughts went through his mind, over and over again.

First get Lorna; then bluff the rest out. With Lorna safe, he could visit the Villa Chalon, challenge the Count, Raoul, Philippe—*was* it the same Philippe?

He went to the balcony. The two men whom Lucille had pointed out were on the promenade, ready to follow him. He had been right to wait until darkness before going to the rue de l'Arbre. He couldn't move the Citroen yet—but must, soon.

He went over the make-up case and everything he would need for a disguise; sooner or later, disguise would be vital.

He went downstairs for lunch, then came to an abrupt halt in the hall.

Two policemen in uniform and a man in plain-clothes stood by the desk. When the head porter sighted Mannering, he pointed, and the three men turned around quickly.

I I

POLICE

As he looked into the pale face of the man in plain-clothes, a dozen fears flashed through Mannering's mind. Among them was the fact that he had talked to the night porter; that he and Lorna had been seen to leave, late at night; that only he had been seen to come back. There were a dozen ways in which the police might have traced him.

The man in plain-clothes, flanked by the uniformed police, had a big face, a heavy jowl and heavily-lidded eyes. He looked as if he had great difficulty in keeping awake—until one got close enough, and noticed the bright shrewdness of those sharp eyes.

"M. Mannering?"

"Yes."

"I am Inspector Flambaud, from the Commissariat de Police."

"My pleasure, m'sieu." Mannering bowed.

"M'sieu," echoed Flambaud. "You are, I understand, the owner of a shop in London and an expert in jewels and other precious things."

"An expert?" Mannering shrugged, deprecatingly. "A dealer, m'sieu."

"You arrived yesterday?"

"That's right."

"M. Mannering, would it be possible for you to extend to me and my colleagues a little assistance?"

"If I can, m'sieu."

"It will be necessary for you to come with us," Flambaud said. "Is it possible for you to come now?"

"As you wish." Mannering was smiling, mechanical.

"You are very kind," said Flambaud. "We shall go, then." He put a hand on Mannering's forearm. It might have been a gesture of friendliness; it might have been a warning.

With Mannering, Flambaud led the way to the front door. One man whom Philippe had sent to watch him sat as if frozen to his chair. Another, across the road, was standing up.

Mannering wished he could enjoy their consternation.

His heart was hammering; fear stormed. But at least Flambaud hadn't gone up to his room, wasn't proposing to search—yet.

Flambaud was cold, aloof, formal. The French police could be unpleasant. Flambaud might know a great deal, might have found something which had proved that Mannering had been to the Villa Chalon—although the villa had not been mentioned. That might simply be to play on Mannering's nerves.

A large Renault was parked outside.

One of the uniformed policemen took the wheel, the other sat by his side. There was good room for Mannering and Flambaud at the back.

Mannering glanced up as he got into the car. Lucille was on the balcony, gripping the rail with both hands, the wrap falling back from her shoulders. It was possible even then to see and to notice the beauty of her figure.

Lucille looked dumbfounded.

She and Philippe would be dismayed; frightened.

And—how would this affect Lorna?

"You will smoke, m'sieu?" Flambaud thrust an open packet of dark-looking cigarettes in front of Mannering's chest. Mannering found most French cigarettes nauseating; but he took one.

Flambaud had a lighter with a flame which looked as

if it would make a beacon by itself; and the black smoke suggested that it had been filled with petrol from the car. Flambaud settled back in his corner and folded his plump hands on his large stomach. Standing, his stomach hadn't seemed so massive; now, it proved to be huge.

"Will this take long?" Mannering asked.

"I cannot tell, m'sieu."

Could disaster have come so swiftly? Mannering tried to think back to the time he had spent at the villa. Had he left something behind which had brought the police straight to him? Some clue, some absurd little thing he hadn't noticed.

They turned off towards the headland, and started to climb.

Mannering fought back fears, looked casually about him. Flambaud gazed out to sea as if nothing interested him more. His hands, the fingers interlaced, laid flat on his stomach. A diamond ring on a finger of his right hand and it sparkled in the sun.

Once out of the town, they drove very fast.

Mannering remembered the wild drive down here the previous evening; the taxi-driver; the quiet beauty; and Lorna's hand on his. Now, he had Flambaud's arm pressing against him. They swung round corners, climbing all the time, until Mannering recognized the corner just before the viewpoint. They swerved round, tyres squealed, drove off the road and on to the parking place, jolting to a stop a few inches from the wall.

"You have been here before, m'sieu?" asked Flambaud.

"Yes."

"When?"

"Last night."

"At what time?"

Mannering said slowly: "I'm not sure. I suppose it

was a little after eleven o'clock. Between then and half-past eleven.''

"What did you see?"

"What *is* there to see?" asked Mannering mildly.

Unexpectedly, Flambaud smiled; he showed small, yellow teeth with wide gaps between them.

"The lights, yes, and what else, m'sieu? Did you meet anyone else here?"

"No."

"So," said Flambaud. He still gave no clue as to his thoughts, but sat with his hands folded loosely, looking out towards the sea. "We will go on, Duval," he said suddenly, and the driver started the engine, swung violently back on to the road, reversed as far as the gates leading to the Villa Chalon, and then drove up—twice as fast as the twisting road justified.

There were a dozen people about the villa, including several policemen.

The car jolted to a standstill.

"M. Mannering," Flambaud said, "you are not compelled to come with me. I request it. I cannot make you come."

He didn't smile, just looked at Mannering from beneath those lazy-looking lashes.

"I'll help where I can," Mannering said.

"Have you been here before?"

"No."

"We will get out," Flambaud said.

Duval opened his door and jumped out, opened the back door and waited for them to get out. Two or three men came towards Flambaud, and he waved them away, testily. They came on and tossed questions at him. To Mannering's surprise, he answered. Two men turned to Mannering; the Press was much the same here as in England.

"You come to help M. l'inspecteur?" asked one.

"Enough!" exclaimed Flambaud. He took Mannering's arm again, thrust his way through the crowd, and approached the back of the villa.

The sun blazed and burned; nothing looked as it had done the night before.

They turned a corner. Two gendarmes stood by the side of the french windows which Mannering had forced. There was no attempt to hide the damage. The pieces of frame which he had cut out were piled against the wall. Sawdust had been brushed up carefully, and was in a small dustpan.

The door was open.

Flambaud looked at the forced window, then at Mannering. His eyes might have been open a fraction more than they had in the car. Mannering looked at him, hoping he seemed puzzled, fighting back the fears which throbbed in his mind. Could he have left anything behind? He hadn't smoked, it couldn't be an English cigarette. He hadn't left prints——

"It looks as if you've a burglary on your hands," he said, and hoped that he sounded casual.

"Yes." Flambaud gave a quick, wintry smile. "A burglary. Come with me, please." He led the way into the passage, then into the front hall. He looked as if he were heading for the library, but instead he turned towards the stairs. Mannering glanced round. Duval and the other uniformed policemen were just behind; he had exchanged the two watchers sent by Philippe for the police.

They went up the stairs.

At the landing, Flambaud stopped. For the first time he gripped Mannering's forearm, instead of touching it lightly. It would be easy to scream at him. The two men halted at the head of the stairs. Two others stood by a closed door.

"M'sieu, you have spent holidays in Chalon before."

"I have not."

"Have you been here?"

"I have driven through several times."

"When you have come to the South of France, m'sieu, where have you stayed?"

"In Nice or Cannes or Juin les Pins, at the Cap——" Mannering shrugged. "Never at Chalon."

"Have you been to this villa before?"

"No."

"You are a friend of the M. le Comte."

"No."

The eyes, half hidden by those drooping lids, were very bright. This wasn't a question of needing help. Flambaud was suspicious, he must have some reasons for that, but the questions gave Mannering no clue.

"You have a friend in England, a Mr. Bernard Dale?" The question came very flatly. Flambaud used the English "Mr." and the present tense.

"I knew Bernard Dale," Mannering said, "but he was murdered, M. l'inspecteur."

"Murdered," echoed Flambaud, and seemed to relish the word. "So I am told." He waved his plump white hand, and the gendarmes by the closed door moved, one to open the door, the other to salute smartly.

"Enter," said Flambaud.

They went in.

Stella Bidot lay on a single bed, with a sheet covering her as far as her neck. Her throat had been cut, and the sheet and pillow were stained with blood which had dried and turned brown.

Flambaud peered at Mannering, had a hand raised, a finger pointing.

12

THE HIDEOUS THREAT

THE finger stabbed.

"You came here, you killed her!" Flambaud accused, and his voice was like a lash. "You came, you killed her!"

Mannering looked at the beauty of the woman who had been Bernard Dale's wife.

"You came, you killed her—you!" The finger stabbed again, was close to Mannering's face.

He turned his head and looked at Flambaud almost contemptuously. Then he moved slowly towards the bed.

She had been lovely indeed. It looked as if she had been sleeping here when someone had stolen upon her and slashed—as swiftly, more swiftly, than Flambaud was now stabbing his finger. She was dressed, wearing a cream linen frock.

"Confess it, Mannering. You came, you killed her. Your name was on a slip of paper in her handbag. She came here to see you. She telephoned you last night, you came here to see her, you——"

"I wasn't here and I didn't kill her." Mannering pushed past the inspector, and went across to the window, looking out upon the bay and the town and, nearer, the grounds with all their beauty, the rioting colours and the restful green of the grass. Not far off a stream trickled down rocks towards the bay; and the sun danced upon the water.

"Why did you do it?" screeched Flambaud.

His voice wasn't so shrill. His bluff had failed, and he knew it. But where shock tactics did not serve the

police, routine might. If Flambaud searched the hotel
room——

Other police might be searching the room now.

"Don't be a fool," Mannering said quietly. "I wasn't
here last night. I'd no reason to kill Stella. She was once
the wife of a friend of mine." It helped to talk; and he
could talk rationally. "Her parents ought to be informed,
and she had a daughter." He pictured little Betty, who
had once screamed and then shivered in silent horror.

He saw Tony Bennett in his mind's eye—within a few
days of being hanged for a murder he hadn't committed.

It would be easy for the wrong man to pay for this
murder, too. If the police could prove that he had been
here . . .

Philippe had.

If Philippe were a murderer, and Lorna was in his
hands . . .

"Have you talked to Scotland Yard about this yet?" he
asked abruptly.

Flambaud hesitated, looked as if he wanted to fling
another accusation, then changed his mind. His little
shrug suggested that he was in a foul temper.

"Not yet."

"Ask them about me," Mannering said.

"I know about you. The dealer, the detective." That
was almost a sneer. "Why did you kill her?"

Mannering said: "I'm not going through that nonsense
again."

"Come with me," the Frenchman said. He gripped
Mannering's arm tightly, and the grip did not suggest that
he had given up hope. They went outside. A gendarme
closed the door and locked it. Flambaud led the way
downstairs and Duval and the other man followed; it
was like a procession. Others stared from the spacious hall,
with its one wide window overlooking the bay; it seemed

as if every window in this house overlooked some part of the bay.

They went into the library.

The bookcases were in their normal position.

Flambaud picked up a telephone, and barked: "Give me l'Hôtel Mirage." He wanted Mannering to know to whom he was speaking. His eyes were wide open now, and he glared.

Outside, two or three of the newspapermen were at the window, doing and saying nothing.

"L'Hôtel Mirage!" roared Flambaud. "This is Flambaud. I wish to speak to Inspector Michel. Quickly, please!" His glare was on Mannering all the time. Then: "Michel, this is Flambaud. What did you find in the room?"

Mannering had fought against believing the worst. Of course, Flambaud had left a man to search the room. If he were good, he would take that light-fitting down. If he had——

There was an agony of waiting.

"You are sure?" Flambaud demanded shrilly. He wasn't pleased; Mannering felt his worst fears fading. Flambaud banged down the receiver, and his glare switched to Mannering. "Wait here, please." He jumped up and stalked off, leaving Mannering with two gendarmes and with the newspapermen at the window.

Flambaud might try again; might feel sure the jewels were in the room. But did they *know* about the jewel theft? Why should they? He was getting confused, jumping to conclusions. Jewels hadn't yet been mentioned.

If the police looked, they could see the marks in the wall made by the bullets fired when he had opened the safe. No one had seen them yet, apparently. There was certainly no evidence that anyone had discovered that the strong-room had been entered.

Flambaud appeared at the window, talking to the newspapermen, waving his arms about. His voice rumbled through into the room but Mannering didn't catch what he said. Then all of the men disappeared and there was only the beauty of the grounds and the sea.

Mannering lit a cigarette and it was half smoked when Flambaud returned. He was smiling; this was only his second smile for Mannering's benefit, and he appeared to be doing his best to look really genial.

"I am sorry to have brought you here and kept you so long, M. Mannering. You have been very helpful." He made no reference at all to his accusation. "Do you wish to return to your hotel?"

"As soon as I can."

"There is a reporter, from *Ce Soir*. The tall man without any hair," Flambaud said casually. "He is returning to Chalon, and will take you, if it is convenient. You see, I have work to do here." He smiled again. His eyes were half closed. "You will not leave Chalon, I may want to see you again." He looked like a fox who knew that one chicken had escaped him and was peering round for another.

His smile faded, and he moved towards the door with Mannering, looking as if he had almost forgotten that Mannering existed.

Mannering reached the front terrace.

A small Citroen came bustling up the drive, as a tall, youthful-looking man, who was absolutely bald, sauntered across from the driveway.

"M. Mannering, I will be happy to drive you into Chalon. Or anywhere you wish to go."

"Chalon, thanks." Mannering smiled at him, and looked at the driver of the bustling Citroen. One glance was enough. This was Lucille's Philippe.

Philippe looked swarthy, angry, vigorous. He jumped

out of the car and slammed the door and then strode towards Flambaud, who was by the front door with a group of gendarmes and other plain-clothes men.

"Philippe Bidot," remarked the reporter from *Ce Soir*. "It will be a shock for him, or it will not surprise him at all!" He smiled. "My name is Monet, M. Mannering."

"You're very good, M. Monet," Mannering said.

Monet was naturally very curious. He knew a little but not much about Mannering's record in England; and about Quinns. He tried to make Mannering "admit" that he had come to Chalon on business, especially to see M. le Comte and his family. He was nonetheless charming because he failed. He drove with care and showed proper respect for every hair-pin bend.

The car drew up outside the Hôtel Mirage.

Lucille was sitting on the terrace. She didn't move when she saw Mannering, but he was quite sure that she was relieved. The two men were also on the terrace, sharing a table.

"Will you come and have a drink?" Mannering asked Monet.

"You are very kind. Later, perhaps, but now I have to telephone to Paris." Monet bowed and shook hands, and went back to the car. Mannering waited until it had driven off, then approached the hotel entrance. Lucille started to get up, but quickly sat down again.

Mannering waited for the lift. Lucille didn't appear.

He got out at the fourth floor, and looked about him. No one was in sight. He caught a glimpse of himself in a long gilt mirror; his expression didn't suggest that he was enjoying life.

He bolted his door when he went inside the room. Then he stared up at the light-fitting. There was nothing to suggest that it had been touched since he had left.

There was a tap at the door.

"Who's there?"

"John, this is Lucille, I would like to see you."

Mannering went to the door and opened it. Lucille looked scared as she slipped past him.

A maid was walking along the passage, saw him, and smiled; was it imagination or was there something strained about that smile?

Lucille now wore dark green; a linen suit.

"What happened, please tell me?"

"Don't you know?"

"First, the police took you away and I was terrified. Then Philippe went rushing off to the villa."

"I saw him, looking as if he were terrified of being hanged. Or is it guillotined here?"

She looked frightened all right; had been frightened for some time. Did she know of Stella's death? Was Philippe the killer—here, and in London?

"You're in bad trouble," Mannering said roughly. The girl's fingers were cool against the back of his hand. "I warned you to be careful from the beginning, didn't I?" He lit a cigarette, striking the match savagely. "Do you know why Philippe went?"

"He got a telephone message and hurried away, looking—as if he could kill."

"As if he *could* kill," Mannering gripped her arms, tightly, shook her. "As if he could or as if he *had* killed? It's time you talked. What's going on here? Do you *want* to be hanged for murder?"

She breathed: "Who—was killed?"

"Stella Bidot."

"Oh, no," Lucille sighed. She seemed to sag, and he let her go. She dropped on to the end of the bed and looked up at him helplessly. "Oh, no, no," she repeated. "Stella was so charming, so kind to me. Not *Stella*."

"I saw her, with her throat cut."

"No," breathed Lucille. It was not so much fear as dread, horror, which crept into the tawny depths of her eyes.

"No," she repeated in the same tone of horror, and shrank away from him. "You did not kill—*Stella*."

Silence came between them. It went on and on, as Lucille looked at him with deepening horror. There was no doubt that, knowing he had raided the Villa Chalon, she thought he had murdered Stella. Her breathing grew short and laboured.

If Philippe talked, fearful of his own danger . . .

Mannering said: "No, I didn't, Lucille. One of your friends did."

She stood up and squeezed past him as if she were afraid to touch him. She went to the door and opened it, went out without looking back. The door closed quietly. Mannering didn't go towards it. He did not know whether she had gone to her own room or not.

He was sure that the news of Stella's murder had taken her completely by surprise. Yet Philippe might have killed the woman. A new field of possibilities was opened up, new dreads, new questions came.

Tony was in deadly danger; the same danger now came close to Mannering. Add the threat to Lorna; add the inevitable questions—*who* had killed Stella, and why?

Why had Stella come back so quickly?

Mannering felt sick with apprehension; greater now because the police might also be watching him. He could try to make Lucille talk only at the risk of having Philippe tell the police about his visit to the villa. He felt as if he were in a vice.

He sent for a snack in his room; it was three o'clock. Darkness seemed as far away as ever, and he could not go to the rue de l'Arbre until after dark.

He was tired, too; he needed sleep. He dozed in an

armchair, then got up in a fury of impatience and went to Lucille's room. There was no answer when he tapped; when he banged. He returned to his own, leaving the door ajar, but did not see or hear Lucille go to hers.

A little after seven o'clock, when dusk was falling, he went again. The passage was empty. He used a picklock, a blade of his knife, and had the door open in a trice. He stepped inside quickly. The room was in darkness and he stretched out a hand to put on the light. Then he stopped, and his arm seemed to go numb.

Horror had already piled on horror. Would there be more?

He pressed the light down, holding his breath.

The room was empty.

He could tell at a glance that Lucille had packed up and left. There was a screwed up cigarette packet; oddments; a sprinkling of face powder on the glass top of the dressing-table, a dozen little indications to show that she had been here; and there was the perfume he had noticed the previous night.

Mannering swung round and went out, slamming the door, hurried downstairs and on to the terrace, which was filled with diners. The orchestra was playing and a crowd had gathered to watch and listen.

Men watched.

Some might be policemen.

In London a man was within a few days of the gallows, and his wife was in despair. Here, Lorna was in the hands of crooks who might be, who probably were, killers. Flambaud was hostile.

Facts were facts; and one which faced him was that he couldn't go on by himself.

Whom could he send for?

He put in a telephone call to Britten's London flat. It came through quickly, but Britten wasn't in. His wife, who sounded as if she were in the next room, promised to tell him at once that Mannering wanted him at Chalon, but would that help in time? At best, Britten couldn't get here until the next day.

Mannering went downstairs, across the terrace and along the street. He had to make sure whether he was followed before he went to the rue de l'Arbre.

The time for the visit had come at last, and he had to work alone.

13

VANISHING TRICK

MANNERING walked through the crowd listening to the orchestra, took a narrow turning, and sauntered along. He did not seem to be followed. He made several detours, watching all the time; neither police nor Philippe's men appeared to be following.

He hurried back to his room. He could put on a disguise, go out, take the Citroen, and at last get to the rue de l'Arbre.

The telephone bell rang.

Mannering swung round towards it, pushing aside the balcony curtains. It rang again before he reached it. He snatched up the receiver.

"Hallo?"

"*Good* evening, Mr. Mannering," said a man with an English voice; a laughing English voice. "I trust I find you well."

Mannering breathed: "Good Lord. Chitty!" Here was the help he needed desperately.

"Chittering, at your service," said the London newspaper man. "And downstairs. Where's the best food in Chalon, John? I'm hungry. I don't eat with my ears, though, I could bear to hear all that's been happening."

"Who knows you're talking to me?" Mannering asked sharply.

"No one, except the operator. The porter was busy, so I helped myself to the house 'phone."

"Good," said Mannering. "Turn left out of the hotel, take the second left after that, and you'll find a restaurant

called *Baccarat.* It's just the name, not a game. I'll meet
you there."

"Very secretive, aren't you?" observed Chittering.
"You wouldn't be on the run by any chance, would you?"

"Take a table by the wall, so that I can sit with my
back to everyone else."

"The mysterious Mr. Mannering," murmured Chittering. "Okay, John."

He rang off.

Mannering went out, and still wasn't followed.

Chittering sat in a far corner of a small, homely
restaurant, his curly, silky hair plastered down for once,
round face beaming; he was something of a gourmet, and
seemed delighted with the food.

"Hallo, John! You certainly know where to eat." They
shook hands. "What's for you? On me—I've plenty of
francs, being on business!"

A waiter hovered.

"Something simple——" Mannering looked down the
menu, and ordered a single meat course. "What business,
Chitty?"

"Stella Bidot."

"When did you get the news?"

"On the tape about midday," said Chittering. "I told
my purblind editor that this was remarkable—ex-wife of
murdered jewel-dealer herself murdered in South of
France where a certain well-known dealer from London
had flown—to wit, John Mannering."

"Who told you that?"

"There was a personage being seen off at the airport,
and our hounds were there," said Chittering. "You were
spotted. I didn't think it was just a holiday, or you would
have said you were going. I was due for a nice soft job,
anyhow, and so I managed to get myself sent here. You
know the line. *Scotland Yard Fails to Find Killer, Daily*

Record Starts Own Hunt In Public Interest." He grinned. "How's Lorna, and what have you been up to?"

Mannering told him, quietly.

For three minutes, Chittering stopped eating. The *patron*, who had shot an occasional benign look towards him, grew anxious and drew nearer. Chittering began to eat slowly, but it was obvious that he was no longer relishing the food.

Mannering finished.

"Well, well," breathed Chittering. He put down his knife and fork. "Not another word from Lorna?"

"No."

"It's just as well I came," Chittering said. "What can I do?"

"Try to find out what's happening to Philippe Bidot. The first thing—find out where he lives, and whether the police know about a house he has in the rue de l'Arbre. The police may have held him. I wouldn't mind knowing more about Lucille Rivière, too," added Mannering.

"Which is most urgent?"

"Whether the police know about rue de l'Arbre."

"O.K.," Chittering said. "I'm staying at the Mirage, too. I'll call you when I've had a chat with the Reuters man here."

"Don't be surprised if I'm away for a night, it won't mean I'm missing."

"What's in your mind ?"

"I might have to vanish," Mannering murmured. "I've a make-up kit with me. I'll daub my face and book a room at a smaller hotel somewhere at the back of the town. If I should have to run for cover, I'll have a safe spot ready for myself."

"Right," said Chittering quietly.

The hotel, the room, everywhere here, seemed empty

to Mannering. Perhaps because he had talked to Chittering and brought normal life nearer, the fact that Lorna was missing hit harder. The night was darkened by the shadows of menace.

He opened the largest case that they had brought with them. Inside was the make-up box, which would not have shamed any star of the London stage. He locked the door, then placed the box on the dressing-table, and adjusted the lights. Satisfied that he couldn't see his reflection more clearly anywhere else, he began to use the make-up.

It changed his looks——

With the lilting strains of the music floating up from the terrace, the noise of passing cars, the knowledge of the listening, watching people, he worked swiftly, expertly. Greasepaint altered his expression and seemed to change the shape of his nose, his eyes. An older man began to peer at that same reflection.

He was completely absorbed in the task, oblivious of sounds, of fears.

He thrust tiny pellets into his nostrils, thickening his nose; worked thin rubber over his teeth, so that their gleaming whiteness was hidden. They looked yellow, and several of them appeared to be stopped with silver. He rubbed oil into his hair then brushed it straight back from his forehead, so that there was no parting; and when he had finished, sat for several seconds, turning his face this way and that.

"Not bad," he said, and glanced at his watch. "Twenty-five minutes. I'll have to make it quicker."

The telephone bell rang. He lifted the receiver quickly. It was Chittering.

"Philippe lives at the Villa Chalon. No one seems to know about the rue de l'Arbre," he said.

"Fine," said Mannering.

He rang off, picked up a small case which he had packed earlier, and went down by the stairs.

Soon he was walking along the narrow street quickly enough, but limping slightly. No one, behind him, would have realized that it was Mannering. The habit of disguise, the knowledge that it went much further than altered features, was part of his life. The way he walked, the way he sat down, even the way in which he put his hands into his pockets or lit a cigarette, were all different.

He had to have a hideaway ready, took the Citroen, and drove along narrow turnings towards the back of the town, where he knew there were small hotels. He chose one called les Trois Couronnes with poor lighting outside and with a dowdy-looking front hall. Madame herself was at the desk, large, powdered, amiable. Mannering's French deceived her. He signed in as Maurice le Brun, and was taken by a small boy to a room on the third floor; there was no lift, and the stairs were steep.

The room had a high ceiling, but was slightly fusty. It had a curiously attractive quality which was hard to place. It was as if he had stepped out of the twentieth century and entered the nineteenth—yet there was a bathroom of sorts. The bed was large, and with a canopy over it; the chairs were like museum pieces. There was a telephone in a corner, by way of further contrast.

The boy went off.

Mannering left, soon afterwards, for the rue de l'Arbre.

14

PHILIPPE

MANNERING drove through the back of the town, struck the sea road and found the rue de l'Arbre. A lamp was alight at one corner, but little light along the rest of it. The houses were terraced, tall, narrow. They opened straight on to the pavement, and there were few places for the police to hide, and only three ways of getting in—from the front, the back or the roof.

Mannering drove slowly along the road.

The yellow headlights showed the houses on either side, the closed shutters, here and there boxes of geraniums at the windows. No one moved, all was quiet.

He saw a man standing in a doorway, some distance along the street; was that a watching policeman or one of Philippe's men? The man was within twenty yards of Number 27, but on the other side of the street. Not far away from him a small light glowed from a wall bracket.

Mannering studied Number 27, seeing the sharply pointed gable, distinguishing it from its neighbours. He drove past, slowed down some distance along, and turned his head. He couldn't see the man, so assumed that he was still in the doorway. It would be wise to assume that he was Flambaud's agent and that the house was being watched.

What about the back?

He knew the planning of these French houses and streets. Each block enclosed a large garden, split into little grass or flowered patches, each owned and tended by the owners of one house. Entry to the gardens was made through courtyards which were deceptive; from the street there were just big wooden doors and, even when opened, only cobbles leading to staircases, both to the right and the left. But beyond these cobbled paths were the gardens.

Round the corner, he saw large wooden doors which were open. Lucille had gone in there.

Round the next corner he left the car and walked back towards the wooden gates. He stepped cautiously over the cobbles, making very little sound. He couldn't see far, although a dim light burned from a bracket on the wall.

He stopped moving abruptly.

A match scraped, then flamed. He saw a face in outline, as the man lit a cigarette.

Flambaud was having Philippe watched; or Philippe had posted guards.

Mannering went back to the car, waited by it until he felt sure that he hadn't been noticed. Then he drove off, until he reached the sea road again. He could hear the now familiar whisper of the sea against the beach. The stars were brilliant and reflected on the bay. Some way out, a pleasure boat was ablaze with colour, and he fancied that he could just hear the strains of music. By the side of the car, he fastened the tool-kit round his waist and wound a length of rope above it.

Finished, he walked to the street, leaving the car pointing towards Chalon.

Another car, with yellow headlights, came from the direction of Cannes, travelling at speed. Eddies of dust curled about Mannering's feet.

He turned the corner and peered along. He couldn't see the man in the doorway, but made sure that no one was approaching before he turned to the outside of the house round the corner. Had Lorna been here, she would have seen the change she knew so well, yet hated. He was transformed—Mannering died away, the Baron took his

place. Even his thinking was different. Here was the
need to break into a house, and it brought excitement
because it meant danger.

The shutters were all closed; there were small iron
balconies and stone window ledges to help him.

He stood on a ledge close to the ground, stretched up
for the first balcony, and pulled himself up.

That was easy.

He stood on it for a moment, peering along the road;
then he started up again. Here a ledge, there the iron-
work of a balcony, there the handle of window shutters,
gave him the hold he wanted.

He didn't look down.

The houses were tall. Half-way up, clinging to the
wall like a fly, he heard the hum of a car engine. He
stopped moving. The car was coming from Chalon at high
speed. He could just make out the yellow glow of the headlights. Unless it turned into the street, there wasn't a
chance that he would be seen.

He heard the tyres squeal. The car swung round the
corner, almost without slackening speed. The light
touched Mannering's legs. If driver or passenger happened to glance up, he would be seen.

The car scorched past, and turned a corner.

Mannering started to climb up again.

It was more difficult as he got nearer the top. The
balconies were smaller up here, and the iron work less
sturdy; once he put a hand on one and a grating noise
came loudly, the steel began to pull away from the
wall.

He eased his weight off it.

He held on to the guttering above his head, and had
the toe of his right foot on a ledge: there was no room for
his left foot. If he slipped, he would fall a hundred feet,
with nothing to break the fall.

He groped cautiously along the guttering. If that cracked or came away, his chances would be negligible.

He forgot everything but the need for getting on to the roof; he *was* the Baron.

He put his weight on his arms and the guttering, gradually. He felt it sag a little, and heard a groan.

Would it hold?

He hung for a moment, with all his weight on the guttering; the moment when disaster could come. But it held. He hauled himself up, grunting with the effort, until he could get an arm on the roof and swing his right leg on to it.

He heaved himself over.

Then he lay spread-eagled on the thick tiles of the sloping roof, breathing heavily, his heart thumping. He felt more fear, now, than when he had been climbing. He lay like that for several minutes, until his breath came more easily. Then he began to climb towards the crown of the roof. He was less nervous of being seen from the street, now; the only danger would come from windows opposite.

He moved cautiously from one roof to another.

On the other side, he could see the gardens, some walled, some serving several of the houses in the four streets which made the square. A light glowed at one of the archways leading into the garden. He thought he saw the red glow of a cigarette, but couldn't be sure.

The light on the wall of the house near Number 27 was getting nearer.

From below, the pointed gable of Number 27 had seemed easy to identify; now, the roofs all looked alike. Mannering tried to picture the scene from below. He had passed the doorway where the man lurked; then the light; then Number 27. And remembered, it had that pointed gable—more sharply pointed than any others he had noticed.

In order to judge, he needed to be further away.

He climbed slowly towards the far side of the roof, and then looked across. The gables showed against the dark sky; and one was sharper than the others.

He smiled freely, elatedly.

Then he looked over the edge of the roof near the garden. The windows on that side were not shuttered, as they were on the street side. So this was his way down. Over the guttering, down to the first balcony, and in through the window. If it opened easily he would get through. If he had to force it, he might be seen by any watching men.

He couldn't see anyone now.

15

THE HOUSE

MANNERING leaned against a square chimney stack, looking down into the garden. He could just make out the shapes of the ground floor windows of the other houses and the doorways which led through to the streets, but at this end there was no light. He waited patiently. Now and again he thought he heard a movement, but couldn't be sure.

Then a door opened, creaking noisily.

Mannering stared down.

A glow of light appeared for a moment, and then faded. The door closed. A moment later, he heard a voice. He couldn't hear the words but it was a man's voice, and there was nothing urgent in the tone.

Another man answered.

Mannering heard no sound, but a match flared; and a moment later two red glows appeared in the darkness.

Angled against the sky, they could see him if they looked up; and there was no way in which he could make sure that they didn't. But they were more likely to be watching the ground floor, not the roof.

Suddenly, footsteps sounded again. The door squeaked, light appeared and faded again; and the door closed for a second time. There was only one man down there now.

The balcony he wanted to reach was just visible. Getting to it would be fairly easy; getting there without alarming the watching man would be a different matter.

Mannering uncoiled the rope round his waist, looped

one end round a chimney stack, tied it securely, and then
tested his weight against it. Next he crawled towards the
edge of the roof, and let down the rope till the slack lay
coiled on the balcony. He turned his back on the waiting
man, the garden and his fears. He lowered himself slowly.
Soon his feet were pressing against the wall, above the
balcony and a little to one side. Most of his weight was
taken by the rope.

He went down inch by inch.

Soon he was far enough down to touch the edge of the
balcony with his right foot. He moved crabwise so that he
could rest his weight on the rail. As he did that cautiously,
there was a faint squeaking noise but nothing else, nothing
that would reach the ears of the man below.

He lowered himself further, then stood on the balcony.

The glass of the window looked dark and shiny; stars
were reflected on it.

The rope would provide a means of escape without
giving a clue to the identity of the burglar if it were found.
He turned and peered down into the garden. He could
see nothing now; the man wasn't smoking.

The danger wasn't past, although he was no longer
visible against the sky.

He turned his back on the watcher, and groped about
the window, until he touched the handle. This was a
french window, opening straight into the room beyond;
probably into a bedroom. There might be someone
sleeping there; one, two or three people. A single shout
would ruin his chances.

He inserted his knife and pressed down the catch. It
squeaked. He pushed the door gently, heart thumping. If
the door were locked, it would increase the risks, every
moment he stood here the danger grew.

The door opened.

He felt a wave of relief, almost of elation, and stopped

pushing. He relaxed for a moment; and only then did he realize how tense he had been. He drew out his whisky flask and took a sip, screwed the cap on quickly, grinned to himself in the darkness, and then pushed the door wider open. It made no sound.

He stepped into the room, took out his pencil torch and switched it on. A beam of light shot out and struck a wall not a few feet ahead of him; he swivelled it round, slowly. Light reflected from the glass of pictures, then from polished furniture. This wasn't a bedroom.

No one was here.

He found the door and stepped into the passage. The floorboards creaked. He stood quite still, shining the torch along. First there was the handrail of the banisters, then a turn at the landing, next the stairs. On the other side of the passage were two doors; another door was straight ahead of him.

If Lorna were at this house, she would probably be on this floor.

Mannering approached the first door, turned the handle and found it unlocked. The trouble now was that he would have to do the same thing at every room; to exert the same caution all the time. Any single moment could be disastrous.

The first room was a bathroom.

The second was an empty bedroom.

The third was a boxroom, filled with cases, trunks, crates, old pictures, oddments which probably had no use at all. So there was no one on this floor.

Mannering turned to the head of the stairs.

The boards creaked; once there was a sharp report, so loud that he stopped quite still; his heart hammered. No one stirred. He reached the next landing, and used the torch to reconnoitre again. This floor also had four rooms, like the one above.

The first was an empty bedroom. He could smell camphor, and saw dustsheets spread over the bed and the furniture. He moved away, closing the door behind him, and then opened the next.

He heard the sound of breathing.

Now he stood very still in the darkness, listening. Someone was asleep in here, but the door had been unlocked; if Lorna were here she would be locked in.

He judged the position of the bed, then went slowly towards it, careful at every step in case he kicked against a chair. Soon, he switched on the torch. It shone on the gleaming auburn of Lucille's hair, on to the honey glow of her forehead.

He turned the torch away from her, and murmured softly: "Clear conscience, Lucille?"

He made sure that no one else was in the room, then went out. The key was in the inside of the lock; he took it, locked Lucille in, and pocketed the key.

Everywhere was silent.

As he opened the next door, he felt disappointment which was taking the edge off his excitement. He wanted a *locked* door, but he had to be sure who was in each room. He listened, but heard no sound of breathing. That wasn't conclusive proof that no one was there. He stepped inside and shone the torch. A made bed was opposite the window. Oddments of women's clothing were flung across this. He swivelled the torch round, and light was reflected from the mirror of a dressing-table. He switched it off quickly; if the man outside saw that, he might begin to wonder.

As the light went out, Mannering caught sight of something which made him stop moving.

He held his breath as he shone the torch again, risking the brightness of the reflection from the mirror.

On the dressing-table was a handbag; Lorna's beyond

any doubt. This was the bag he had given her just before he had left her at the car and started for the Villa Chalon.

Mannering went slowly across the room towards the window. He didn't look out, but stretched up and pulled the curtains. He made more noise than was necessary; his first careless moment. He turned and stepped quickly towards the door, switched on the main light, and then closed the door.

Yes, it was Lorna's bag. He went across the opened it. Her fountain pen—the one she had used when writing the note—powder compact, lipstick, note-case and purse; all the familiar things were there. The note-case was full of francs, they hadn't robbed her.

Nothing else of hers was here.

Where had they taken her?

Mannering put out the light and stepped into the passage. Lucille would know; and it should be easier to make Lucille talk than any of the others. He had to know.

Was it worth looking in the other rooms? There were two more on this floor, others on the floors below; each one might be used as a cell for Lorna. But if she were in another room, why was her handbag here?

He turned to the rooms he had not yet visited; the first was unlocked. He heard the sound of breathing inside. The torch light shone on two beds and an elderly couple, facing each other. Mannering locked them in.

He had to find Philippe.

The next door was locked.

He stood very still, fingers clutching the handle, making sure that it wasn't just jammed. He knew that it was not. He drew back, listened intently, hearing no sound from above or below. Hope flared back, driving away that feeling of disaster. If he had found her, he must make sure he couldn't have victory turned into defeat; he must find the men.

He turned away abruptly, and went downstairs. The floorboards here were sturdier and he made hardly a sound. On the landing, the carpet was thicker, silence was easy. The passages were wider, too. Mannering used the torch freely, and found three rooms instead of four; the first was a library, the second empty, the third a bedroom with Philippe Bidot asleep in the large double bed.

Mannering switched the torch off as soon as he recognized Philippe, who turned in his sleep. There was a momentary break in his even breathing. Mannering went nearer the bed.

Philippe was dangerous and might be deadly; remember that.

Close to the bed Mannering shone the torch again, to make sure that he could judge the distance properly. Then, in the darkness, he curled his fingers and gripped Philippe's neck.

For a moment there was no movement, no hint of resistance; then he felt the man take in a sharp breath. Philippe's body stiffened, then moved in one convulsive effort to get free. Fingers clutched at Mannering's wrists, fastening round them like claws.

Mannering's hands were tight about the man's throat.

Philippe's legs thrashed the bedclothes, he tried to tear himself free, his fingers clawed—but that was only for a few moments. His struggles slackened.

Mannering eased the pressure slightly, and Philippe made another convulsive effort to free himself, but hadn't a chance.

He became slack; unconscious.

Mannering shone the torch round the room. Heavy curtains were drawn, if he switched on the light it wasn't likely to be seen from outside. He switched it on, then turned to the unconscious Frenchman. Lying with his head on one side and his lips slack, the swarthy handsomeness of the man still showed. His dark hair curled a little, and his black lashes swept his cheeks.

Mannering tore strips off a linen sheet, bound Philippe's wrists, then flung back the sheet and bound his ankles. He pulled the blankets up, tucked them in firmly and tied the rest of the sheet across Philippe's chest and round under the bed. Philippe was stirring; before long he would come round. Mannering gagged him, next, and then went quickly through the pockets of his clothes, which hung on a stand by the foot of the bed—coat on a padded hanger, trousers stretched to ensure a perfect crease. He found the automatic pistol in the pocket of the coat and a bunch of keys. Then he searched the room swiftly, but found nothing else that he thought might help, except for a door-key which was lying on the dressing-table.

By then Philippe was conscious, and staring at him.

Mannering worked without saying a word. Philippe's gaze followed him everywhere. Deliberately, and in spite of the urgent summons from the locked room upstairs, Mannering stayed longer than was necessary. Then he turned and looked into the dark bright eyes of the man on the bed.

He took the pistol from his pocket, watching Philippe closely. The bold eyes narrowed, but Philippe made no attempt to speak through the gag.

Mannering went out, switching off the light as he went. The torchlight showed him the way upstairs. He was satisfied that no one else was in the house—except in that locked room.

Philippe's keys jangled. Mannering reached the locked door, took out the key which he had found on Philippe's dressing-table and slipped it into the lock. Had he guessed right? Was it the key of this door? His hand shook so that he could scarcely turn it, but it did turn.

He thrust the door open and stepped into the room.

16

FAILURE

THE beam of the torch shone straight towards the bed in a corner of the room, and fell upon Lorna's face.

Relief was like a flood; mental and physical, relief which killed all other thought and feeling.

Mannering stood with the torch shaking a little, but the beam still showed every feature, and Lorna's dark hair, She was asleep. She did not seem to be in any pain, and her arms appeared to be free.

Mannering closed the door behind him and moved across the room. Then he had to go back, to switch on the light. The shutters were closed at the window, no one outside would know that the light had gone on. It was dim, but good enough for him to see more clearly.

Lorna lay in bed, turned towards Mannering and the door, one arm beneath her, the other, bare to the shoulder, hanging over the side of the bed. For the first time, Mannering thought that she was lying awkwardly.

Her hair was untidy and she had on no make up; she looked peaceful; *too* peaceful?

"All right, my darling," he said, and reached her.

Then he saw why she lay like that. There was an iron bracelet round her left wrist, and the bracelet was chained to the post at the foot of the bed. She had some freedom of movement, but couldn't get free. Mannering felt his teeth grating as he went down on one knee.

"Lorna," he whispered, "wake up."

She didn't stir.

"Wake up, my sweet." He kissed her cheek and gripped her wrist—the wrist which was free from the bracelet and the chain.

"*Lorna!*" he said, and his voice broke.

Swift, dark fear attacked him; but she was breathing; he could see movement at her lips and at her breast. The frilly lace of her brassiere showed, but her arms and shoulders were bare. He gripped her shoulders and shook her, suddenly fierce.

"Lorna!"

She did not stir.

Mannering drew back, then raised one eyelid gently. The pupil of the eye was just a tiny pin-point, hardly visible. She had been drugged, probably with morphia; and from the look of her she would be unconscious for hours.

It was useless to try to wake her.

He took Philippe's keys out of his pocket, selected a small one which might fit the bracelet, and turned it in the lock. That fell off her wrist. There were only slight marks on the flesh; nothing suggested that she had been ill-treated.

He moved her so that she was lying on her back, both arms quite free. He pulled down the sheet and light blanket. She wore just a brassiere, a pair of panties and a suspender-belt. He glanced round; the dress she had been wearing when they had gone together to the Villa Chalon was draped over the back of a chair, her shoes were on the floor. He picked up the dress, it buttoned all down the front, so he was able to get her into it. He put on her shoes and then he left her lying on the bed, looking peaceful and comfortable.

He waited for a moment on the landing and took another sip of whisky, then lit a cigarette and went down to Philippe's room.

The man's eyes widened as he went in, and Mannering guessed something of his tension.

He drew deeply at the cigarette, and went across the room. He kept his eyes narrowed; he was quite sure that the disguise was good enough to fool anyone, especially in this light. He drew at the cigarette until it burned very red, then, by the side of the bed, took it out and looked at the glowing tip.

"This can burn," he said, in thick guttural French. He put the cigarette to his lips again, and then took out his knife. The sharp blade flashed.

Philippe did not flinch even when the knife drooped towards his face.

Mannering cut the gag free; it fell to one side. Deep marks showed on either side of Philippe's lips, but they were not angry or painful. His eyes looked their questions, seemed to ask:

"Who are *you*?"

Mannering said: "Where did you stab Stella Bidot?" He moved the knife, point downwards, and pricked Philippe on the chest; then he took the knife higher. Philippe's eyes followed it until the point and the blade were out of his sight, hidden by his own chin.

Mannering pressed the back of the blade sharply against the man's skin. It did not cut; it could not have hurt; but Philippe started violently.

"That's right," Mannering said. "Only when you cut her throat, you didn't tell her what you were going to do, did you?"

"I did not kill!"

"You killed her," Mannering said, "and the police know you did. Shall I send for them? Or would you rather they didn't come in and find Mannering's wife a prisoner?"

Philippe somehow found his voice.

"Who—are you?"

"Mannering's quite a person," Mannering went on, and his voice was very harsh. "He gets mad at times. If he knew where his wife was, he'd get mad at you. Why did you kidnap her?"

Philippe didn't speak.

"You'll have to find the answers," Mannering said. He didn't grin, didn't gloat. His face was blank most of the time and when he spoke his lips hardly moved. It would all heighten the effect, increase the other's fear. "Why did you kidnap her? What's Mannering done to you?"

"He—he robbed—Villa Chalon." Philippe tried to move, it was almost pathetic. "You're wrong. I didn't kill Stella. Mannering killed her."

Mannering didn't speak.

"I tell you he killed her!" Philippe said hoarsely. "I——"

He stopped abruptly. His eyes darted to and fro, as if quite suddenly he was desperately afraid to meet Mannering's eyes. He moistened his lips. "It was not I. Mannering broke into the Villa Chalon, he——"

Mannering grinned. The light showed the silvered stopping of the fake teeth, gave him a dark and sinister look; one of sly menace.

The knife seemed to slip; it nicked the side of the Frenchman's neck. Philippe winced, and tried to see it, as if his eyes could keep it away.

Mannering gave another sneering grin.

"I want two answers. Why did you kill Stella Bidot, and why did you take Mannering's wife away? The answers had better be good. Don't take me wrong," Mannering went on, and looked again at the glowing end of the cigarette. "*I* don't mind you killing Stella. I just want to know what made it worth your while. And what

have you got against Mannering? Tell me, Bidot. I've
been wanting to cut Mannering's throat for a long time,
perhaps I can fix him now." He paused, then added
softly: "Perhaps you'd even swear to the police that
Mannering raided the villa. That would finish him.
Will you do that?"

If he convinced Bidot that he and Mannering were
two different people, and that "he" wanted to see
Mannering dead, the man might talk.

He *had* to talk. . . .

Mannering moved the knife in front of Philippe's eyes.
"Will you tell the police about the burglary?"

Philippe didn't answer, and it was easy to understand
why. If he told the police that, he would be telling them
about the hoard of stolen goods still at the villa.

Mannering said viciously:

"So you won't. You're afraid of the police discovering
the strong-room. Before you can risk that, you must empty
the room, and you can't do that until the police clear out.
You've been too clever, Bidot. I'll tell you something else.
I could whisper about the strong-room to the police.
Flambaud is looking for something like that. What I don't
understand is why you killed your sister-in-law . . ." he
switched to that abruptly.

Philippe's expression changed. Fear faded into astonish-
ment—then into amusement. Mannering knew that he
had got something wrong—so wrong that Philippe was
so relieved that he could smile.

"You fool," Philippe said. "You can guess what you
like, but——"

He stopped abruptly. A sharp, buzzing sound cut
across his words, coming from the wall near the bed.
Alarm drove the fierce gleam out of his eyes.

"What's that?" Mannering asked sharply.

"An alarm bell," Philippe said promptly. "I have

5

guards outside, one is raising the alarm. It may be—the police."

Or it might be that a guard had discovered that Mannering was in the house.

Mannering turned round abruptly, and hurried to the door. He heard footsteps as he stood by it, covering Philippe with the Frenchman's own gun.

"*Quiet!*"

The footsteps drew nearer.

Mannering opened the door, and called sharply:

"What is it?"

"The police, m'sieu," the man gasped as he reached the landing. "They are watching, one has gone to the back and taken Marcel away. I was not seen. Now, the house is watched, back and front."

He reached the room.

Mannering smashed a blow on to the back of his head. He fell, with hardly a sound.

17

LUCILLE OBEYS

MANNERING went out on to the landing. Behind him both men were bound and gagged; helpless. The house was silent. He made his way to Lucille's door and listened, then unlocked the door and went in: Lucille was still sleeping, on her side, face towards him. He put on a light, sat down on the side of the bed and placed his left hand over her mouth.

She started violently; her eyes fluttered open.

"Keep quiet," he said softly. "Don't move." His voice was still harsh and rough; back in the past he had cultivated the trick of altering its timbre, so as to make a disguise foolproof.

Lucille lay very still; terrified, her great, tawny eyes turned towards him. He kept his hand on her mouth long enough to make her really frightened, then said:

"I shall kill you if you make any noise."

He took his hand away. Her lips were parted, and her teeth showed, giving some indication of her terror. She made no sound, except for her laboured breathing. He stood up and moved away.

"Get up."

"Who——"

"Get *up*!"

She flung the bedclothes back. It reminded him of the way she had climbed out of his bed the first time he had seen her. She had been full of confidence then; now, she was quivering with fright. She wore a pair of pale, peach-coloured pyjamas, high at the neck.

"Get dressed," he said sharply.

"What——"

"Do as you're told."

She obeyed him hurriedly; he kept to one side of the room, his back towards her. Had she approached him he would have known. Presently she called to him nervously:

"I'm ... I'm ... ready."

Mannering turned round. "Can you drive a car?"

"I—yes, yes, of course."

"You will go along this road till you get to the sea-front, there you will turn right, and under the first lamp post you will find an old Citroen. Here's the key." He handed it to her. "You will drive the car straight back here. Is that clear?"

"Yes, but——"

"Now, listen." He had to make sure of her obedience. "If you don't come back with that car, something will happen to Philippe, something that won't be pleasant."

"I—I will do as you say,"

"Mind you do. And listen again—you may see some-one outside. Take no notice of them."

"Who——"

"Just take no notice."

He went downstairs with her and opened the front door silently. Lucille slipped through, Mannering closed it again and hurried into a front room. He saw a man, undoubtedly a police watcher, come out from a doorway and stare up the street after Lucille. Evidently the man had been instructed not to go far from his post.

He walked across the road, shining his torch at the front door. In a moment Mannering was back in the hall. He unfastened the door, and let it swing slowly open, keeping well behind it. He heard the man come up the steps and call out:

"Is anyone there?"

He entered the hall. As he did so, Mannering caught him a tremendous clip on the back of the head. He pitched forward, hitting the floor with a thud. Mannering was on him in a moment, but he was quite unconscious.

Mannering dragged him into the front room, and locked the door.

He hurried upstairs, collected Lorna's bag and then went to Lorna's room. He hoisted her over his shoulder, fireman fashion, and made his way slowly downstairs. In the hall he propped Lorna on a chair by a small table on which was a telephone. He noted the telephone number, then went to the door to listen. He could hear nothing, so he turned off the light and opened the door; as he did so, a car turned the corner. It might not be the Citroen, Mannering realized; it might be more police.

The car stopped and Lucille got out. She came up the steps. He swung the door wide open, and stood blocking her view of Lorna.

"Go straight up to Philippe," he said. "You'll find him all right. No lights!" he added, as her hand went towards the switch.

He waited until she had turned the bend in the stairs, then picked Lorna up and carried her out to the car. No one was in sight. He drove round the block and out to the shore road again, where he pulled up by a telephone kiosk. There he telephoned the Hôtel Mirage. The answer was prompt enough, but when he asked for Chittering he had a long wait. Then a brisk voice came on the line.

"M'sieu, I regret to inform you that M. Chittering has left. Is that M. Mannering?"

Mannering said heavily: "Yes." He had been relying on the reporter, needing help desperately.

"He was recalled to his office," the man said. "It was some big news in London. But your other friend is here, M. Mannering. I have been able to give him the room next to yours."

Mannering said: "What other friend?"

"Surely you expected M. Britten?"

Mannering gulped. He had forgotten Dick, who might be better even than Chittering. There was still hope.

"I—yes," he said. "Yes, I was expecting him."

Dick hadn't lost any time; was as anxious to find the killer as he. He would probably have news of Tony Bennett, and his wife.

"Would you like to speak to him, m'sieu?"

"Please."

Britten was soon on the line, eager, even a little edgy.

"John, where are you?"

"Never mind. I——"

"I'm up-to-date, Chittering told me everything before he left. Have you found Lorna?"

"Yes," said Mannering. "I think she's all right, except for dope. Listen, Dick. Get a taxi, and come to the second seat along the shore road, beyond a turning called the rue de l'Arbre. You can't miss it—it's a couple of turnings past a street with a white house at the corner. Got all that?"

"Yes."

"Take Lorna away, and if you think she needs a doctor——"

"I'll do what's necessary," Britten said. " 'Bye."

Mannering hung up, and walked back to the car. He drove into a side street, and waited. He had to make sure no more police arrived before Lorna was safe.

After ten minutes, he drove up to the seat, lifted Lorna out and settled her on it. Then he drove back to the side road, and watched. Other cars came near, on other roads; engines stopped suddenly, voices were carried on the quiet night.

The police were at 27, rue de l'Arbre in strength.

He didn't try to guess how they had discovered the house or why they were there. They'd gone from the heart of the town, not by the sea, or they would have seen him.

Should he take Lorna away before they started searching?

He saw a car; it slowed down, and stopped by the seat. Then in the street light he saw Britten and the driver lift Lorna into the taxi.

When the taxi had turned and disappeared, Mannering drove his car to a public parking place near the Trois Couronnes. Ten minutes later he was on the telephone to Britten.

"How is she, Dick?"

"She'll do. Sleeping off some dope, and I don't think she needs a doctor. But where *are* you, what——"

"I'm all right," Mannering said. "I'll be seeing you." He rang off and hurried to the small hotel. A sleepy night-porter nodded to him. He went up to his room, with a dozen thoughts crowding his mind.

He wouldn't talk to Britten or to anyone yet. He had to get more rest. He could do the wrong thing too easily. Lorna was safe, he was beginning to have hopes that things would go well, and a man he was sure was innocent would be saved from the gallows. Philippe was a danger; the police offered as great a danger. But now he had those jewels and could use them as a bargaining weapon because Lorna was safe. Dick would look after her. Good old Dick! Bless his heart for coming so quickly.

It would be easy to become light-hearted.

Mannering took off his clothes, and flung them over a

chair. He began to yawn, and couldn't stop. At last he
dropped into bed, turned over and looked towards the
window. He pictured Lorna's face. With luck she would
hardly remember what had happened. Soon they would
be able to laugh together.

Questions came, sharply. *Who* had killed Stella?

Who had killed Bernard Dale?

Would Flambaud get proof that Mannering had been
to the villa on the night of the murder?

He slept.

When he woke up, a gentle breeze was blowing in at
the open window, and the cream lace curtains shivered a
little in it. Unfamiliar sounds came in at the open
window, from the street and the nearby market.

He yawned.

After ten minutes or so, when everything that had
happened had come back to his mind, he got out of bed,
and pressed a bell-push set in the wall by the fireplace.
There was at least a chance that it wouldn't work.

A little maid with a look of the country about her,
tapped at the door and came in nervously.

Mannering ordered coffee and *croissants*, then went
into the tiny bathroom, where the bath was little more
than a tub. But the water ran hot. He couldn't shave and
didn't want to until he knew how long it would be before
he could safely reappear as Mannering.

The coffee was good and the rolls delicious.

It was half-past eleven when he went to the telephone,
and called Britten.

Britten might be out.

He was in, and unexpectedly brusque.

"I've been sitting with my ear glued to the telephone
for the past hour," he growled. "You mustn't come back
here."

Mannering felt tension gripping him again.

"Why not?"

"This policeman Flambaud is on the rampage. He wants to see you again."

"Any idea why?"

"No, John. Sorry. He does not look upon English solicitors with much favour. I told him you were out," Britten went on briskly. "As far as I can judge, he doesn't think much of Englishmen anyhow! Lorna's not come round yet, but I didn't get a doctor. Her pulse is better, nothing to worry about."

"Has Flambaud asked to see her?"

"He's seen her—and he'll worry her with questions as soon as he can. I'm being as difficult as I can with him, one of the reasons why I'm not too popular. Who are you at the moment, by the way? Mannering or this le Brun Chittering told me about?"

"Le Brun."

"I should stay that way for a bit. Where are you?"

"The Trois Couronnes." Mannering paused. "Any hope of finding out what Flambaud thinks he's got on me? Has he arrested Philippe Bidot or Lucille Rivière, do you know?"

"I'll find out, if I can. You stay where you are, but give me your telephone number."

Mannering gave it and rang off, moved across to the window and looked down on the throng of people going towards the market. He hardly noticed them as they walked along with their laden baskets, with their long loaves under their arms, the women brisk and smart, the men casual. He hardly noticed the blaring horns and the snorting motor-cycles and the ringing of the cycle bells. He kept seeing a mind picture of Flambaud.

If Philippe had talked, it would explain a rampaging detective; but would Philippe dare to talk? Wasn't he far more likely to be terrified in case the police discovered what had been in the strong-room? Why had he laughed when Mannering had talked about that? Wasn't Philippe worried about what the police found there?

There was another possibility—that Lucille had cracked under police questioning.

Mannering took out a little notebook, found the telephone number of the house on the rue de l'Arbre, and called it. There was no answer for some time; then a frail voice answered—it might have belonged to an old man or an old woman.

"M. Philippe Bidot, please."

"He is not here."

"Then I will speak to Mam'selle Rivière."

"A moment, please, sir."

Mannering waited, and the moment proved a long one. Then he heard odd sounds at the other end of the telephone, and Lucille spoke quietly—so subdued that he wondered if it were the girl.

"Mam'selle Lucille Rivière?"

"Yes, m'sieu.'

"You will recall that we met last night," said Mannering briskly. "You were good enough to fetch my car for me. Will you——"

"*You* are the man who took——" she almost screamed.

"Yes, I am the man," Mannering said. "I shall be at the Café d'Or in twenty minutes' time. You know where that is, of course. Meet me there by yourself—without being followed by the police."

"I could, but——"

"Or I shall call Flambaud and tell him that Philippe was at the villa when Stella was killed," Mannering said harshly.

He rang off.

He couldn't be sure that the threat would bring Lucille. But until he knew more, until he could find the murderer, that danger hovered over Tony Bennett. With Lorna free, Mannering could act——

But he had the stolen jewels; a false move would put him in acute danger.

18

THE CAFÉ D'OR

THE sun gleamed on the gilt umbrellas of the Café d'Or. It was two hundred yards away from the Mirage, a small and exclusive restaurant and café. Chairs, tables, mirrors and doorways all had their share of gilt, and every waitress had hair so brightly yellow that it looked as if they had been trying to imitate the sun.

Mannering sat at a small café, two doors along, with a glass of beer in front of him.

He saw Lucille some way off, and something of his tension eased.

She wore the lemon-coloured sleeveless dress. It would be easy, watching her, to think only of her figure, her shapely arms, the ease of her graceful movements. Instead, he watched the pavement behind her. He did not think that she was followed, but he waited until she reached the café, making sure that no one came and sat nearby.

Lucille looked about her anxiously, and waved a waiter away. She lit a cigarette and drew on it deeply, still glancing swiftly right and left.

Mannering joined her.

She took the cigarette from her lips and looked at him agitatedly.

"What happened last night?" Mannering demanded.

"After—after you had gone, m'sieu?"

"I have some knowledge of what happened while I was there." The sneer was intended to sting.

"Yes—yes, m'sieu." She looked at him frankly, but

there was fear in her eyes. When she had first come to him she had been brimful of confidence. It had been hard to see her as bad, in the sense of evil; but she had been very sure of herself. Danger to herself and Philippe had changed all that.

"There was a man who said our door was open and he had been knocked senseless in our hall and locked in the dining-room," Lucille said. "When he came to, he climbed out of the window and fetched more police, who were watching at the back. Still more came. I said you had made me dress and forced me to fetch a car. I didn't know the number and didn't notice the make."

"And did that satisfy them?"

"*Satisfy* them?" She shook her head vigorously. "Not for one moment. It was not long before Flambaud arrived." She looked out to sea; and Mannering could tell what she thought of Flambaud; he had terrified her. "He would not believe that anyone had broken into the house. I was not until he found the rope tied to the chimney that he believed us."

"Us?"

"He talked also to Philippe," Lucille went on. "I had released him. It was—it was a terrible time."

Mannering said: "I can believe it." His eyes, narrowed so that she would have less chance to recognize them, were on her all the time. There wasn't a blemish to her skin. "Did you tell them about Mrs. Mannering?"

"No."

She was scared; so was Philippe.

"Did Philippe describe me to the police?"

"We both said that it was to dark in the room to see you properly."

"And was Flambaud satisfied then?"

"I would not say that he was satisfied," said Lucille, "but he could not prove that it was untrue. Finding the rope told him that you—you had come in from the roof. He switched his anger on the men who had been watching the house." A glimmering of a smile curved her lips. "That was something to hear, m'sieu!"

"Where is Philippe Bidot now?"

"He has gone to the Villa Chalon," Lucille said. "His uncle and his brother will be there soon."

After a pause, Mannering said:

"What is he to you, Lucille?"

A glow sprang to the tawny coloured eyes.

"We are lovers," she said; and there was pride in her voice. "We shall soon be married."

"Do you think he killed Stella Bidot?" he asked abruptly.

"No!"

"Then why are you frightened?"

She said slowly: "Because Philippe was at the Villa Chalon *when* she was murdered. It was Mannering who killed her, but Philippe——" she broke off, biting her lip.

"Who says that it was Mannering?"

She didn't answer.

"Philippe?" Mannering asked abruptly.

"It must have been Mannering!"

"What of his brother, Raoul?" said Mannering, changing the subject abruptly. "Do you know him well?"

"Very well."

"Are you sure that he has been in England?"

"I am quite sure," Lucille said. "Yesterday he telephoned from London. Philippe also telephoned to Raoul in London. It is so tragic for Raoul, he——" she closed her eyes. "He was so much in love with Stella."

"Was she in love with him?"

"When she first came here they were very happy. Then she was not so happy, it was as if she was thinking about her first husband. But it was not until after he died that

she—she alarmed Raoul. For the first time he began to
fear that she was falling out of love with him."

"Did he guess why?"

"No," Lucille said gravely, "no." She opened her
handbag and took out another cigarette, then leaned forward for a light. "Why do you ask all these questions?"

"Remember that I know that Philippe was at the Villa
Chalon." Mannering paused. "Lucille, what would you
say if you *knew* that Philippe had killed Stella?"

"Don't say it!" she exclaimed.

"You're beginning to think that he did, aren't you?"
Mannering watched her intently, seeing the fear filling
her eyes. He was sure that she was in love with Philippe;
as sure that she was beginning to think it possible that
Philippe had murdered Stella. "Do you know that he is
a thief? That he deals in stolen goods, jewels which"—
he was going to add—"have blood on them," thinking of
the Gramercys, but she didn't give him a chance to finish.

"Oh, *that*," she said abruptly, and waved her hands as
if it could not matter less. "He takes from fat pigs of men
and fat pigs of women—what do they matter? I will tell
you something, m'sieu. He takes from those who have too
much and gives to those who have too little. He is a good
man, but——"

Mannering didn't speak, but his change of expression
stopped her. He saw part of the truth, so obvious now
that it was hard to believe that he hadn't seen it before.

"Did Philippe plan to *rob* the villa?"

Lucille didn't answer.

"Is that it? Or when he saw a thief there, did he mean
to collar the jewels for his precious poor? Come on,
let's have the truth."

"I do not have to——"

"I'll find proof that he was at the villa. You're playing
with his life."

She said slowly, almost proudly:

"Yes, m'sieu, you are right. His rich uncle with his paltry gifts to charity, is a thief. At the Villa Chalon there is a hoard of stolen jewels, other stolen valuables, *objets d'art*. There was a great opportunity to get some of these on the night Mannering arrived. It was thought that Mannering might break in seeking some special jewels. Then Philippe——" she broke off.

"Who warned Philippe that Mannering was coming and might break in?" Mannering asked abruptly.

"I do not know."

"Who was it?"

"I tell you I don't know!"

He found himself believing her; but he would soon find out the answer. He would have to; meanwhile, he could guess.

Who could it have been but Stella? But why should Stella——

Lucille went on:

"Philippe was going to steal the jewels—some of which he *knows* are stolen—and Mannering, or an unknown, would have been blamed. It did not go as Philippe planned—Mannering saved the jewels. But Philippe had taken away his wife, and——" she broke off.

"So it didn't work out," Mannering interrupted, as if talk of Lorna didn't matter. "And now Philippe's at the villa, under suspicion of murder."

"He did not kill her!"

"I hope that's true," Mannering said. "When he comes back, tell him to expect a visit from me."

He stood up, and left her.

No one followed him.

She watched from the table. He walked briskly to the other side of the road and past the Hôtel Mirage; nothing had changed there, he saw no police about. He crossed the road again, entered the foyer and went straight to the lift. The liftman who knew him well as Mannering, showed no sign of recognition.

"Fourth floor, please." Mannering stood on one side, and the lift crawled upwards.

The door of Mannering's room was locked. He tapped, but there was no answer; so Lorna wasn't conscious. He went to the room next door, but there was no answer from Britten. He returned to his own door, took his penknife out of his pocket, opened the picklock blade, and a few seconds later was inside the bedroom, looking down at Lorna.

She was sleeping peacefully, and had lost much of the night's pallor. Someone had brushed her hair and washed her face, so that it was free from lipstick and make-up. She looked so restful, so far from fear, that it was almost hurtful to stand and look down at her.

He heard a sound at the door. It might be Britten, might be the maid. He swung towards the balcony and reached it before the door opened.

He watched——

Britten came in, his fair hair almost white, his face slightly red with sunburn. He wore a light grey linen suit, just right for the weather.

He approached the bed, glanced at Lorna, and said quietly: "Waking up yet, old girl?" Lorna didn't move. "Won't do you any harm to sleep a bit longer," Britten said to himself, and lit a cigarette. "I wonder how you'll take it, if anything should go wrong with——"

He stopped abruptly.

Mannering heard his voice but didn't see him. Britten's abrupt silence made him realize that he had been seen. He moved forward, grinning—and found himself looking into the muzzle of a gun.

"All right, Dick," Mannering said in his natural voice.

"What the hell——" began Britten, and then gulped. "Good lord! You put the wind up me." He gulped, and dropped the gun into his pocket, came forward quickly. "You're *ask*ing for trouble. Flambaud——"

"Won't recognize me," Mannering said.

"I shouldn't take too much for granted." Britten offered cigarettes, and added with a grin which was more tense than usual: "You'd better have a drink, too, you'll need it." He turned back to the room, and Mannering followed. "I've just come from the Villa Chalon. As Stella's brother, I was able to get in. Not that I know any of the others well. God! I'd like to strangle the man who——"

Mannering said quietly: "I can guess how you feel. But the only thing we can do for Stella is to avenge her. We can still save Tony."

"How?" Britten's voice was sharp. "What do you mean? John, you haven't——"

"I haven't proved a thing," Mannering said, "but it's easy to believe that the same man killed Bernard and Stella. If we can find him, Tony's safe. If we could only find a motive, we'd be nearly home."

"The man killed Dale, of course, because he caught him at the safe," said Britten. "But I can't see any reason for killing Stella."

"Possibly she discovered who Dale's murderer was."

"How could she, she wasn't even in England at the time?"

Mannering shrugged his shoulders.

"We'd better stop guessing. Who's at the villa now?" he asked.

"The Count and Raoul are back. Philippe's there, too—and Flambaud joined them. If we could really make that trio talk we'd probably get somewhere." Britten scowled at the blue mirror of the sea. "John, I'm scared.

It was bad enough before. But to-day Philippe threw *your* name into the conversation. He said Flambaud ought to get you, you're the killer."

Mannering didn't speak.

"I'm pretty sure that one of those three killed Stella," Britten went on, "and may have killed Bernard, too. But think of the danger. Tony's already condemned, remember, they'll hang him. If they get you too——" he broke off.

"They haven't a chance," Mannering said, but he felt the cold wind of fear.

After a long pause, Britten said: "Well, you'll beat the odds if anyone can, but don't underrate the risk. Flambaud's reckoned to be a brilliant detective, and the Count is such a big-wig that Flambaud wants quick results. They'll do their damnedest to switch the thing on to you—Philippe's already had a good try. If Flambaud could put his hands on John Mannering at the moment, take it from me he'd arrest him first and ask the questions afterwards."

"Probably. You try to keep the police away from Lorna," Mannering said dryly. He took some things out of his make-up box and put them into his pockets.

"Be careful," Britten said. "Anything I can do?"

"Just stand by," said Mannering.

He went down to the street and got into the Renault. Parked in the sun, it was baking hot. He wound down the windows and drove fast, cooling the car down. Soon he was on the way towards the headland, but he didn't go at once to the Villa Chalon. He turned off a narrow road, parked the car, then walked some distance over the rough ground, until he came to a small quarry with heaps of sandy soil in it.

He took out Philippe Bidot's gun, wrapped rag from the car round it to muffle the reports, then fired it twice into a

heap of sand. He strolled to the sand and began to sieve
it through his fingers, searching for the bullets. When he
found them, he took out a magnifying glass and studied
the marking on them. Now and again he looked at the
ballistics report from Scotland Yard.

This wasn't the gun with which Bernard Dale had been
shot.

19

LIONS' DEN

MANNERING went back to the car.

The reports had been well muffled, he doubted if anyone had heard them. No one appeared, except on the road which he could see a long way below him. Cars passed, most of them crawling, several stopping at the viewpoint which showed them the glowing beauty of the bay.

Mannering took the car further up this road.

Before long, he was able to see the Villa Chalon, although there was no motor road to it, from here. He took out the oddments he had brought from his make-up box, tipped down the driving mirror, removed the nose pads and teeth-coverings and began to clean off the make-up. He used spirit daubed on with a small sponge; after two or three applications, the greasepaint was gone. He took out a tube of shaving cream, and shaved, combed his hair. Then he got out of the car, and started to climb towards the Villa Chalon.

He soon reached the grounds.

A gendarme stood at the gate, looking bored with life; there didn't appear to be one at the front door. Mannering cut across the drive, and saw a man repairing the window which he had forced.

A maid answered his ring.

"I am sorry, m'sieu," she said earnestly, "M. le Comte is not at home."

"Tell him that John Mannering would like to see him," Mannering said.

"But, m'sieu——"

"All right," Mannering said, "I'll tell him myself."

He moved past the maid, and into the now familiar hall. He saw open doors, and heard voices in the big book-lined room. He heard the maid following him, but she wasn't sure what to do. She let him go ahead, without calling out.

He reached the doorway.

Philippe stood against a window, erect, handsome, eyes glittering—obviously furious. His brother Raoul sat at a corner of the large desk. He was fairer than Philippe, handsome but in a less vigorous and dashing way—just a good-looking man who might well be stricken with grief.

Behind the desk sat M. le Comte de Chalon. In morning coat and striped trousers, he appeared more distinguished, less of an old roué, than he had at the London night-club. There was an almost sinister look about him.

Raoul was saying: "What is there we can do? If we betray this Mannering, we shall have to tell Flambaud everything. Now that we know that Uncle has stolen jewels here . . ."

"What runs in your veins?" demanded Philippe. "Is it blood or is it water? Stella was murdered, do you understand? A man drove a knife——"

"For God's sake, stop talking like that!" Raoul cried.

"It is the only way to talk, to make you understand what we have to do." Philippe strode towards the desk. "Uncle, you can surely understand——"

"You know," said Mannering apologetically, "I seem to have come at a delicate moment."

He moved into the room.

The maid rushed after him.

"I told him that you were not to be disturbed, M. le Comte. He would not listen to me!"

None of the Frenchmen moved; they seemed petrified.

After a moment, the Count murmured: "It is all right, Lisette," and the maid went out.

Mannering closed the door after her, and then turned the key in it. He strolled towards the desk, keeping his hands in sight.

Philippe moved, flashed towards him, hands raised and clenched.

"You have the impudence to come here! You, who killed Stella, who——" words seemed to choke him. For a moment it looked as if he would be able to keep back his rage, but it was too much for him. He smashed a blow at Mannering's chin, swung another as Mannering swayed away from the first. The second blow caught Mannering on the shoulder.

"Philippe!" roared the old man.

Raoul jumped to his feet.

Mannering said: "You're always asking for trouble, Philippe." He caught the Frenchman's wrist, twisted, and held it tightly. Philippe was locked in a grip from which he couldn't escape; his body was bent almost double, and the rage blazing from his eyes didn't help him.

Mannering let him go.

"The room seems to be full of people who didn't kill Madame Bidot," he said dryly.

Raoul, approaching him slowly, looked as if he would be more deadly than Philippe; that he would prefer to use a knife than fists. He had altered since Mannering had met him on that first hurried trip here; he looked older. There was hatred in his eyes, and it reflected in the eyes of the man at the desk.

Philippe moved abruptly, getting between Mannering and the door.

"Why have you come here?" Raoul demanded softly.

Mannering said: "I thought we might try to find out

what's been happening," He took a cigarette from a box on the desk. "I don't know what you have in your strong-room, M. le Comte, but apparently it would give the police a shock." His tone hardly changed. "I did not kill Stella. Why should I?"

None of the others spoke.

"I felt pretty sure that Philippe did, as he was the only one of the party present at the time," Mannering went on.

Even Philippe said nothing.

"I suppose," Mannering continued very softly, "there was no jealousy between your nephews, M. le Comte. I understand that there appeared to be some weakening of Stella's devotion to Raoul. If it were possible——"

"Throw him out of here!" rasped Philippe.

"After all," Mannering said, "if the brothers were jealous, it could explain murder. Or if someone else were jealous of Philippe, that would serve. Obviously this could have been a *crime passionel.*" His smile seemed lazy, his manner nonchalant but he didn't miss a single move-ment or expression in any of the other men. "Who would be jealous of an *affaire* between Philippe and Stella, I wonder?"

Philippe raised a clenched hand—then dropped it and spoke quickly, urgently, to his brother.

"It is not true, Raoul." There was appeal in his voice; pleading that he should be believed. It seemed to Manner-ing that the suspicion must have been voiced before, that he had struck a line which was not new to them.

Raoul said: "The very idea is absurd."

"Very brotherly," murmured Mannering. "I hope it's true. But even if there wasn't anything between Philippe and Stella, someone else might have imagined an *affaire* Perhaps there were grounds for suspicion, and someone was persuaded. Who would you think of, Philippe? Not little Lucille, of course."

Philippe spun round.

"Only a dog would suggest it!"

"You killed my wife," Raoul Bidot said, very quietly. There was no anger or rage in his eyes but there was a glow as of hatred. "And one day I shall kill you, Mannering, but not now. When you are considering other things, when you think that there is no danger, then——"

"Tell me *why* you think I killed her," Mannering invited. "Explain my motive."

"You are a thief, and she discovered it," Raoul said coldly. "You broke into this house——"

"Or she discovered that your uncle owned stolen jewels," Mannering interrupted. "Did *you* know that?"

Raoul didn't speak.

"No," said the Count quietly. "Raoul did not know until to-day, that I collect precious stones as a miser collects gold, M. Mannering. A man like you will understand the passion, the mania for them. I can say to you, for no one would believe it if you repeated the story, that I acquire jewels in any way I can. I will buy, I will gladly buy stolen gems, if the price is right." The old man smiled faintly; he had increased in stature, was a character few could match. "You heard as much when you came in. You will know, however, that the mania stops at acquiring precious stones. I had the Gramercys, but Philippe discovered it, and——"

"Did Stella?" snapped Mannering.

"I do not think so," the Count said.

But Stella had; and she had been afraid that Raoul was a thief; she need not have worried.

Here was the wealthy old man who bought stolen jewels—as many did—and was quite self-possessed and unashamed about it. Here was Raoul, the nephew who knew nothing of that; and Philippe, the fiery, daring knight-errant. If Lucille could be believed, he had been standing by and waiting his chance to get into the strong-room—so as to sell the gems and give them away as alms!

Mannering said: "Philippe, who told you I was coming here?"

"My uncle telephoned me from London."

Mannering swung round to de Chalon.

"How did you know?"

"Stella told me it was likely, when she came back from seeing you in Chelsea." The old man smiled faintly. "I knew she had been out, and persuaded her to tell me the truth. So I warned Philippe to keep a most careful watch here. He was not careful enough. Where are my jewels, Mannering?"

Raoul burst out: "Does it matter now? Who killed Stella? Who——"

"Steady," murmured Mannering. "Losing our heads won't help. Finding Stella's murderer without causing a lot of other trouble is our job, isn't it? Can't we work together on that and argue the rest out later? I liked Stella, I liked her first husband. The same person may have killed both. Possibly Lucille is still a suspect. Philippe certainly is. If it comes to that, Raoul would have had time to fly here, kill Stella, and fly back to London. So would you, M. le Comte. That's how the police will be thinking, anyhow. The more you let them think it, the greater the chance that they will want to find out what you keep at this house. If you'd work together and with me, to find the killer, we might get somewhere and preserve your reputations."

"I almost believe you are right." The Count looked very old as he sat back in the chair, his frail hands moving on the polished surface of the desk; but he was admiring; and he mattered. "I almost believe that we have made a mistake, that you know nothing about the murder."

"Don't let him make a fool of you," Philippe growled.

"Either the two murders were connected, and one was the consequence of the other, or Stella was killed for a completely different reason from Bernard," Mannering said. "If we could find the motive, we could probably find the killer. I want to find Bernard Dale's killer because an innocent man might be hanged for the murder. The reason for Dale's murder looked obvious at the time—robbery with violence. The killer stole the Gramercy jewels, remember. Who did you buy them from, M. le Comte?"

"An associate in Paris," the old man said frankly. "Neither he nor I worries *how* we get the jewels, provided we get them. Yes, I am quite shameless. *I* did not kill. But I think it is a waste of time trying to prove that the two murders had connected motives. If you did not kill Stella——" he looked from one nephew to the other, spread his hands over the desk. "All I know is that *I* did not."

Finding out from whom he had bought the jewels was vital for Tony; but making him talk would have to come later.

After a long pause, Raoul said: "Philippe, have you talked to Lucille about this?"

"No, and I will not!"

Raoul shrugged.

Mannering said: "Philippe and Lucille were the only two of you here on the night that Stella was killed, if you're satisfied that none of the servants was concerned."

"The police are fully satisfied that they knew nothing about it'," de Chalon said.

"You are the great detective, Mannering," Philippe jeered. "*You* find out. You find a way of proving that it wasn't you."

"That's exactly what I mean to do," Mannering said.

"One of you killed her. Or Lucille. Or an unknown. I'll find out who it was before I've finished." He swung round and went towards the door, unlocked it, and went out.

He was half-way across the hall when the front door opened. The maid glanced over her shoulder at him, as Flambaud stepped through.

Mannering had heard no ringing, had not dreamed that the policeman was here. He stood quite still. Flambaud moved in slowly, and there were two policemen with him. He held his hands clasped together just in front of his stomach, and there was a glint in his half-closed eyes.

"Ah, M. Mannering, so we meet again!" he said, and strode past him into the library.

One of the gendarmes stopped, and Mannering turned and went back. Flambaud waited until the two gendarmes were in the room, then moved briskly across to Philippe.

"So," he said. "M. le Comte, I am sorry to cause you such distress. M. Raoul, I could wish that my duty was much more pleasant." He slid his hand into and out of his pocket; handcuffs glinted. "It is my duty to arrest M. Philippe Bidot. A passing motorist, of his acquaintance, has just come forward to say he saw him leaving these grounds late on the night of the murder. I have checked at his garage, and his car was out till two o'clock. Yet he lied and said he had never left home. He sometimes uses a motor-cycle, which was seen here, also. Take him away," he said to the gendarmes.

They took Philippe by the arms and started for the door.

He thrust them aside, a swift movement which caught them by surprise. Even Flambaud was startled. Philippe made for the door, as a gendarme out there yelled:

"Stop, there, stop!"

The other two were rushing towards the door, Flambaud after them. There was a thud in the hall, then the crash of breaking glass.

Mannering didn't move, but Raoul and the old man ran towards the door.

Through the window, Mannering saw Philippe racing across the garden, with police streaming after him. Flambaud made a bad fourth. Philippe disappeared behind an outcrop of rock; and the sound of thudding footsteps faded.

Mannering waited for the old man and Raoul to come back.

Raoul said: "We shall have to tell the police everything, Uncle, if they do not release Philippe, if there should appear to be any danger that he will be convicted." Hatred smouldered in his eyes. "I do not think you have much time, Mannering. Whatever it costs us, even if my uncle's freedom and the family's good name are lost, we shall save Philippe's life."

He looked out of the window.

Not far away, Mannering saw Philippe being hustled along the drive between two gendarmes. He was cut off by a police car for a moment, then pushed into it. Flambaud climbed in beside him, and the car moved off.

"You have very little time," Raoul said. "If you did not kill her, find out who did. To save the life of their adored Philippe, all the servants here will swear that they saw you. And Philippe—" he shrugged—"he will now be eager to tell them everything he knows."

The old man said:

"Your word would not carry against ours and that of our servants, Mannering. Nothing you can *say* will help you. Not even the jewels, which you have somewhere. I

agree with Raoul. To save Philippe, I will tell the whole
truth. If you did *not* kill Stella——"

"He killed her," Raoul said bitterly.

Mannering turned towards the door.

20

ADVICE

No one followed Mannering as he drove down the corniche towards Chalon. No one had taken any interest in him when he had left the house.

There was a parking space near the hotel. He pulled the Renault in beneath a tree which would keep it cool for the next two or three hours, lit a cigarette, and stared at the sea. Still no one took any notice of him, except the head waiter of the Mirage, who saw and recognized him.

Mannering got out.

"I am very glad to see you again, m'sieu," beamed the head waiter.

"Thanks," said Mannering. "Had to go away for a day. Urgent business." He smiled, vaguely, and went into the hotel. The porters looked as pleased as the waiter. The lift man smiled widely, and hoped that he had had a good journey. "Very," said Mannering.

He went along to his room, and tapped. There was no answer. He picked the lock, with as little trouble as if he had a key, and went in.

Lorna was saying from the balcony: "We're bound to hear soon."

"Of course," said Britten, "and starving yourself won't help him."

Mannering reached the window.

The linen shade was down, and it was cool. The table was between the two, and Lorna's plate was hardly touched, while Britten's was empty. Lorna looked pale, and she was frowning. Otherwise she showed no sign of the ordeal. If Mannering hadn't driven so close to the hotel, she would have seen him arrive, for she was looking down at the road; hoping.

"Eating would help me, too," Mannering murmured.

Lorna swung round in her chair. Britten half rose from his. Mannering forced gaiety into his eyes as he went forward.

He could feel the thumping of Lorna's heart; the warm softness of her body.

He heard Britten's chair scrape; and thought that Britten went off the balcony.

They stayed like that for a long time; then Lorna's body relaxed. Mannering straightened up, and leaned against the edge of the balcony. There was a film of tears in Lorna's eyes, but she had more colour now. The traffic kept up its continual dirge of sound, and beneath them there was constant movement, but up here there was only the silence and the bond which had always held them together.

"Getting hungrier?" Mannering asked dryly. He bent down and kissed her forehead. "I'm famished. What's the gloom about?"

"Don't pretend that it isn't deadly," Lorna said. But her eyes were brighter. "I can't believe that it will go too far, but—Dick's really worried."

"Flambaud's scared him. There wasn't any need to be scared, Flambaud isn't the man to be scared of," Mannering went on mildly. "He's arrested Philippe. Has Dick told you about Philippe?"

Lorna said: "Yes." But her expression answered for her. "Has Philippe——"

"He's kept quiet as far as I know," said Mannering. "It seems to be a kind of family agreement. All for one and one for all. Did you hear that, Dick?"

Britten appeared at the windows.

"Yes, and it's serious. If they've arrested Philippe, he'll spill everything to save his own neck. You must get away, John, and leave me to sort this out."

"Disguise myself again and disappear?" said Mannering. "Is that what you mean?"

"Yes, until it blows over."

"There's a big snag."

"What's that?"

"Tony's still under sentence of death. I'm now more sure than ever that he didn't steal the Gramercys. The only way out is to find the murderer. It might be wise for me to do a vanishing trick while I'm looking for him, there isn't much time."

Britten said: "John, you were the one who decided to start this thing, you know. The moment you broke into that strong-room, you weighted the scales against yourself. It's no use crying over spilt milk, and no use blaming anyone else. The situation exists, and you've got to meet it. Your position is nearly as bad as Tony's. If Philippe swears that you were at the villa, that's it. The whole story can be pretty well substantiated. Flambaud knows you were near, on the night of the murder. Not fools, these police!" Britten didn't smile; his eyes were bleak. "I tell you that if the French police once get their maulers on you, you're going to have a bad time. They don't work our way, you know—over here you're assumed guilty until you're proved innocent. Don't let them catch you. And even when you become le Brun, don't stick your neck out. Keep away from Lorna. Work very quietly."

Mannering said: "Where would you start working?"

Britten shrugged.

"This is a gospel of gloom," Mannering said, and tried in vain to make himself sound flippant. "And I'm still hungry! I'll eat first and decide what to do afterwards. I'm still a long way from sure that Philippe will talk."

"Are you?" Lorna asked. It was difficult to meet her eyes and to lie.

"Yes.'"

"You know that sooner or later he'll talk," Lorna said, almost impatiently. "The only hope is to find the murderer quickly—or hide."

He knew just how much she hated saying that.

"And we'll move mountains to help," Britten said.

Lorna lay on the bed, two square pillows behind her back, her legs drawn up. She watched Mannering as he sat at the mirror, with the make-up box on the dressing-table. He was changing in front of her eyes; changing more swiftly and in some ways more effectively than he had when he had been by himself.

It was nearly four o'clock.

Now and again, Mannering looked across at her, seeing the fear and the distress in her eyes. She hated the need for going to earth as much as he; but she was desperately afraid; and every time a car drew up outside the hotel, she glanced towards the balcony as if wondering if this were Flambaud.

Mannering worked the rubber covering over his teeth.

"Every time I see you do that, I think you're quicker." Lorna forced herself to speak brightly. "Is the Trois Couronnes comfortable?"

"Homely's the word."

"Darling——"

"Hm-hm."

"I know what you feel. I've never known you say so little. It's almost as if——" she broke off.

"I've a premonition," Mannering grinned. "Not quite as bad as that, my sweet!" But it was surprisingly near it; he felt more despondent than he could remember.

"I feel hellish about Tony. I can't just show the

Gramercys to the police—it would put the rope round my neck too. So I have to find out who took them from Bernard. It might have been any of the trio at the villa, although I don't think Raoul's likely. The old man certainly is. He's one of the ruthless, amoral type, and loves jewels as if they were beautiful women. He knows himself, and he knows who killed Bernard. Stella heard him and Phillippe quarrelling over the Gramercys, and that might mean——"

He broke off.

"He sounds pretty cold-blooded," Lorna said.

"That's the Count," agreed Mannering.

He forced a smile, finished off the disguise, and began to put the greasepaint away.

"I'll do that," Lorna said, getting off the bed. "I want you to get off, darling, I——"

Footsteps sounded in the passage—those of two or three men. Lorna lost all her colour. Her fingers bit so deeply into Mannering's hand that they hurt.

The men passed.

"I just feel that you haven't a second to spare," she said abruptly. "Telephone when you can, and I'll get messages to you. Don't——"

The telephone bell jarred out, making Lorna start violently. Mannering went to the bedside table, affected by her tension much more than he liked.

"Hallo?"

"Hurry," Britten said sharply. "Flambaud and several gendarmes have just arrived. Philippe's free—some sort of alibi for the time Stella was killed."

He rang off.

Mannering put the receiver down. Lorna seemed to sense what the news was. Mannering took her in his arms, held her for a tumultuous moment, then pushed past her. He didn't look back.

He stepped into the passage, fighting to convince himself that he was safe in the disguise. 'He didn't. From the moment he had left the Villa Chalon, he had felt like this —as if disaster were at his heels. There seemed no way out; no clue. If there were one, he had missed it. The obvious things, that one of the Bidots or even Lucille had killed Stella, crowded other thoughts out of his mind. He couldn't see any hope of proving that one of them had.

He knew as little about the true motives now as he had when he had left England.

He hurried down the stairs. The police were crowding into the lift when he reached the ground floor. His heart thumped as he saw Flambaud. The detective's mouth was set tightly, his chin thrust forward aggressively.

Britten was at one of the tables on the terrace. He didn't move or show any sign of recognition; it was as if he were afraid of someone penetrating the disguise. A waiter looked intently at Mannering, then away.

Two gendarmes were near Mannering's Renault; near enough to pounce if Mannering or anyone else should approach it. Mannering walked past them, fighting down the temptation to run. He gave the Citroen a miss, too. He reached the corner. No one looked after him. He walked as far as the main street, then entered a small hotel and went straight to the telephone and called the house in the rue de l'Arbre.

Lucille wasn't in.

There was a possibility, just an outside possibility, that she would be able to help; she might know something which, if disclosed, could point to the truth. But the release of Philippe worsened the situation. As he walked towards the Trois Couronnes, he found himself thinking of Raoul's obvious suspicion about his brother. *Had* there been an *affaire* between Philippe and Stella? Was Philippe fighting desperately for his own life? Had he killed Stella? Or had Raoul? The old man.

Even Lucille killed——

Mannering reached the hotel. Madame, behind the little desk, smiled at him graciously. He went up the steep stairs. The room had been tidied, and there was a smell of lavender; some had been burnt in here recently. He dropped down into one of the old-fashioned but comfortable armchairs.

What could he do?

The one relief was that he had found this hiding place in good time. He could relax without fear that the police were on his heels. But he wanted to do more than relax, he wanted to work, to search——

He lit a cigarette.

The first thing to do was let this settle in his mind. There was still time to save Tony—but no reason for believing that he could. In the morning, he might see angles which he'd missed. Britten might see others. Lorna—the chief anxiety was Lorna. She had seemed almost too worried; desperately afraid. They had been up against it before; the shadow of death and of the gallows had loomed over him. She had never given him the impression of being so deeply afraid, almost convinced that this would be fatal.

21

DEAD END

MANNERING hesitated before he went across to the telephone. Only Lorna and Britten knew that he was here. He hadn't expected a call from either of them as quickly as this. He lifted the receiver, and used the voice of le Brun to answer.

"Hallo? This is Maurice le Brun."

"So it is Maurice le Brun," a man said, and rang off.

There was no doubt of the sneer in the voice; no doubt that he hung up. He had a French accent, smooth, natural.

Mannering looked at the receiver stupidly, then put it down and moved away.

So someone else knew he was here.

The afternoon street was much quieter from this window. He saw two gendarmes with the white batons of traffic police, walking leisurely along the road towards the cinema; a policeman was on duty at these crossroads by day. They disappeared. There was a possibility that they were coming here, but he didn't think about it; he thought only about that man's sneering:

"So it is Maurice le Brun."

Lucille or Philippe might have seen through the disguise; or at least guessed. Either might have set someone to watch him. It was never possible to be absolutely sure that he hadn't been followed.

He must move in a hurry. The police would soon be on the way—unless the caller simply wanted to wear at his nerves.

He kept looking at the silent telephone as he packed his bag, looking out of the window from time to time. If the police came, they would come that way. They might send others to watch the back, but they would come to the front entrance also.

No one arrived.

Finished, he hurried down the stairs, paid his bill, was give another benign smile by Madame, walked rapidly along the main street. He had seen a group of small holiday hotels nearer the headland; his luggage would get him a room, but he hadn't much money left.

He would have to borrow from Britten; and see him again soon.

The buoyant, confident Britten had become frightened; the calm assurance of Lorna had been destroyed. Mannering's own confidence in himself was at its lowest ebb.

He made himself hurry, although there was no hurry—he really had nowhere to go, no idea what to do next. It had been like that almost from the beginning of this case. A sudden spurt of action, temporary success—and a dead end. Dead end, dead end, dead end; and none so dead as this.

He walked along by the little hotels, opposite the smiling sea, within sight of the headland and Chalon's villa. Children's clothes hung at the windows of several of them, swimsuits and bathing caps at others. There were little front doors, most of them in need of paint, all of them closed. He chose a door with pink paint; l'hotel Belle View.

There was no difficulty; he could have a second floor room at the front; *en pension* was very cheap. He booked for bed and breakfast, and stayed for half an hour, before leaving.

He found himself walking towards the Hôtel Mirage; the last place he should go.

He went into a hotel foyer and used the telephone. The Mirage answered promptly enough.

"Mrs. Mannering, please, in Room 407."

"Mrs. Mannering is not here, sir."

Mannering just stopped himself from saying: "Don't be silly." Instead, he said: "Will you please ring her room." She might have gone out, she might have gone anywhere.

"I am sorry, m'sieu, Mrs. Mannering is not here."

"Do you know when she will be back?"

"I have no idea, m'sieu."

Mannering didn't hang up. Something in the tone of the operator's voice worried him more than it should. The emphasis she put on the words, even the phrasing: not that Lorna had gone out, but that she was not there.

"It's important that I should know," Mannering said.

"In that case, m'sieu, I should telephone the police station," the operator said. "She left with M. Flambaud."

Mannering didn't speak; just hung up.

He could see what had happened as clearly as if he had been there at the time. Flambaud had torn into the hotel, stormed up to the room, and, when he couldn't find Mannering, had taken Lorna. Why was Flambaud so sure he was involved? Why had he been, from the beginning?

Mannering left the telephone.

He was a hundred yards away before he realized that he should have asked for Britten. Surely Britten would be able to do *some*thing with the police.

Mannering walked across the road, made himself stand against the railings of the promenade and look out to sea. The lovely scene was unchanged; the gently rolling waves and the swimmers and the splashing children, the gay umbrellas, the sun-bathers in their *Bikinis*, the rustle of water against the grey pebbles. There was the headland, too, and the air so clear that he could pick out the Villa Chalon.

He knew that he could easily panic.

He crossed the road again, called the hotel, and asked for Britten, who was in his room.

"Dick," Mannering said in English, "I need some money urgently."

"I've sent 25,000 francs to the Trois Couronnes," Britten said. "Didn't take it myself in case I'm followed. The police know that we're acquainted. Better not telephone too often, and now——"

"Dick——" began Mannering.

"Let's call it a day, John. I'll be in touch——"

"What's happened with Lorna?" Mannering exploded.

There was a short pause; then Britten seemed to sigh. He spoke again very slowly:

"Flambaud took her off for questioning. I don't think you need worry too much. He's a tough customer, but with Lorna——" Britten broke off. "I've been to the British Consul, and he's promised to get in touch with the Embassy in Paris if there should be anything to worry about. I'm on the spot, John. You keep out of the way for a bit. That's vital, you know—in his present mood Flambaud mustn't catch you."

"No, I suppose not," Mannering said heavily. "Is there anything——"

"For the love of Mike, ring off! The whole world might be listening in!" Britten almost shouted, and then immediately dropped his voice. "Sorry, John. I'm a bit on edge, too. They can listen in so easily. If Flambaud grabs me, we'll all be in a worse mess than ever. I'll be seeing you."

"Yes," said Mannering. "All right, Dick."

There was Tony Bennett; and his despairing wife; Lorna, and his own fears.

He went into the sunlight again. There were a thousand people within sight, and he felt as if he were alone. Britten was right, he couldn't be blamed for shouting; but it had brought the plight home sharply.

The world was full of Lorna—and she was at the Commissariat de Police, being questioned, brow-beaten, perhaps threatened by Flambaud.

The police didn't know him as le Brun, but he couldn't regard himself as safe, because Lucille and Philippe had seen him.

Why was he so barren of ideas? It had been like that from the beginning.

Until Stella had come to London, he hadn't a clue. Why had Stella visited him? Had she told the truth? Why had she told the Count so much, and warned him of the danger?

Why had she come to Chalon?

Here he was, back at the old circle, the old questions.

If there were any connection between the two crimes, why had the second been necessary? What had changed?

He became rigid.

He saw only the shimmering sea and the distant headland, and, far beyond that, the faint line of the horizon. It took a long time to get to some things, but at last he was at this one. There had been a really significant thing happen for the first time since Bernard Dale's death. Stella had visited London; and Stella had come to the Chelsea flat. Soon afterwards she had hurried to the Villa Chalon. She couldn't have been sure, but she might have guessed that Mannering would go there. She might have gone there hoping to see him, with more to tell.

Guesswork?

It was all he had left, now.

The strongest possible motive for her murder was that

she had known who had the Gramercys; unless she had found out who had killed Bernard.

He hadn't yet tackled the old man on his own—or Raoul, who could look so deadly. Again, he had to wait for darkness. There was a risk that the police would still keep a close watch on the villa, but he had to take a chance. If they really thought that Philippe was their man, they might not worry much about the villa.

He would have to get in, tackle the Count and Raoul—and afterwards Lucille.

He needed another car but couldn't get one; he doubted if Britten could provide enough money for that. The money at the Trois Couronnes had to be collected, and that meant a risk—because the unknown man had sneered on the telephone: "So it is M. le Brun."

He began to walk in the direction of the headland; he would have to get a taxi out there, later on; unless there was a bus.

The hotel would tell him.

He began to walk along the narrow streets towards the Trois Couronnes. It was possible that the police had got on to him already, that the man who had sneered "so it is Maurice le Brun' had told them. But if he had, why had he warned Mannering?

Was it safe to take a chance?

He reached the cinema where huge posters showed Betty Grable's smiling face and dancing legs. No gendarmes were near the hotel. He strolled along the street towards it. He could see inside from the pavement, and would be able to tell if a gendarme were in the hall.

He saw no one.

He stepped into the roadway, fears flooding his mind again.

"*M'sieu!*" a woman shouted at him.

A child screamed.

A man roared.

Mannering looked round, and saw the car leaping at him. It was coming round the corner by the cinema, was only a few yards away. He couldn't see the driver clearly.

He leapt.

He felt the car brush against him, then catch his coat. He was spun round, and flung against the window of a shop. He heard the boom as he thudded against the glass. He struck his head, but didn't lose consciousness. He slid down the window to the pavement. He knew that men and women were hurrying towards him. He felt little pain, except an ache in his head—but panic surged until it was a screaming dread in his mind.

This might mean hospital—doctors—nurses—he could not get through all that with the disguise. He must get up, and convince them that he didn't need any help. He felt men touch him, heard voices, managed to struggle to his feet and muttered in English: "I'm all right," and then realized that he had given himself away as an Englishman.

Then he heard a woman say:

"It was a crime. Did you see it, Leonida? The man in that car, he tried to kill the gentleman. That was no accident. Did you see it, Leonida?"

A gendarme was forcing his way through the crowd.

22

THE BACK DOOR

EVEN the sight of the gendarme did not rid Mannering of the shock of the woman's cry: "That was no accident." He heard her voice without distinguishing the words. Others chimed in, some agreeing, some refuting, some laughing. A fierce argument started, while two men helped Mannering to his feet. The gendarme, his white baton swinging, came up importantly.

"Have the goodness to tell me what happened, m'sieu."

"Have the goodness to have some sense." A new voice rasped in the gendarme's ear. "Madame" of the Trois Couronnes arrived, large, purposeful. "M. le Brun is staying with me, he needs rest. Come and see him afterwards, if you must." She hustled the helpful men aside and placed a large, flabby arm round Mannering's waist. Her voice became soft, almost gentle. "Lean against me, m'sieu, it will not be long. We will get you to a couch."

Mannering's head was aching, and the shock was still on him; the near "accident" and the arrival of the gendarme took some facing. The little policeman argued without much heart, as Madame and a man helped Mannering into the hotel.

He shied at the thought of the steep stairs.

"This way, m'sieu," Madame said.

There was a room on the ground floor, dark because the Venetian blinds were drawn; it was a relief to be out of the bright sunlight. Madame helped him on to a soft couch, ushered the helpful man out, spoke sharply to the gendarme at the door, and closed the door in his face.

She approached Mannering, smiling.

"How do you feel now, m'sieu? Is there anything I can get for you?"

"If I could just rest, Madame."

"But of course! I will bring you some coffee, afterwards you shall rest."

She went out, skirts rustling.

Mannering lit a cigarette.

He could hear the clatter of the traffic and the chatter of the crowd outside. The gendarme was doubtless asking questions by the dozen. The woman was probably telling him that the car had deliberately tried to run Mannering down. Had it? He hadn't been thinking, had probably been careless, but he thought that car had swung round the corner very swiftly. A reckless driver was just as likely as a would-be killer.

Who would want to run him down?

Madame brought in the coffee, stirred in plenty of sugar, put a luxurious down cushion beneath Mannering's head, and left him again.

Could he take it for granted that Philippe, Lucille or Raoul knew where he was? If they did, would they tell the police? Would anyone try to run him down one moment, and betray him to the police the next?

He got up, pulled the couch towards the window, and drew the blinds so that he could see out without being seen. The crowd had thinned, but there were three gendarmes instead of one. They would soon be here. Probably only the fierce championship of Madame had kept them out. In the shade of the room he was much safer than outside.

He heard a tap at the door.

Madame peered in, saw where he was, and relaxed.

"It is all right, m'sieu, to put a telephone call through to you?"

Mannering said": Yes. Yes, of course." He stood up and went across to the telephone. He felt and looked much better. Madame beamed, and went out.

He could see two of the gendarmes, close to the windows, as he picked up the receiver.

"Hallo?"

"M. le Brun," a man said in French. "You should get away from there as soon as you can. Flambaud is on his way."

Mannering moved towards the window, reached it, and saw that there were six or seven gendarmes in sight, not all of them with their white batons. He felt the old, familiar feeling of suffocation.

The hotel was surrounded; Flambaud must have sent men ahead of him.

Mannering went to the door.

Madame was busy with a man and a woman at the desk. The porter was waiting to attend to them. Mannering slipped to one side, and was seen by none of them. He passed the foot of the stairs, then went through a doorway on the right.

There must be a back way out.

The door led into a spotless kitchen, where two elderly women and a middle-aged man were busy at the tables and the stoves.

One of the women glanced up and saw him, and said calmly:

"M'sieu, I regret that you are not allowed in here."

"I won't stay a moment." Mannering was apologetic. "Where is the other way out, madame?"

All three stopped what they were doing and looked at him.

"*Voici*, m'sieu," the woman said, and pointed towards a door in the far corner of the room. "Why should m'sieu wish to go out the back way?"

"It is necessary to check the precautions you take against fire," Mannering said. He smiled and bowed and hurried across to the door. It opened into a store-room, there were large refrigerators, shelves laden with wine, bins filled with vegetables. Beyond this he could see the narrow side street.

At the corner, a gendarme stood twirling his baton, and Mannering saw the revolver in his holster. Mannering turned in the other direction. He expected a shout, a whistle, running footsteps. He heard nothing. A few yards along an alley led to the courtyard of a house. He went in, quickly. It was like so many others—the court-yard served several houses in a block. He crossed this, and three minutes after he had left the hotel, he was in the street by the cinema.

Betty Grable beamed down at him.

A Renault swung along the road, and brakes squealed; the signal which heralded Flambaud. He didn't see the detective, but in a few seconds, heard his voice. A police-man on the other side of the road disappeared; Flambaud had obviously called him.

So the messenger had known what he was talking about.

Mannering reached the corner, and glanced to the left. Flambaud and several gendarmes were entering the hotel. Other police stayed on guard. Mannering turned away and walked briskly towards the sea. Except for his aching head and a few bruises, he was all right; but he had come within a foot or two of being squashed beneath that car; within minutes of being caught by Flambaud.

He hadn't much time left.

Flambaud would get a description from Madame, if he

hadn't one already; and Flambaud would work furiously to catch him.

Mannering reached the boulevard; he was as safe among the holiday crowds as anywhere. He turned towards the small hotels, and half an hour after leaving the Trois Couronnes he was in his room at the Belle View Hotel, overlooking the bay.

He had the tool-kit round his waist; a few thousand francs that would last him for a day or two at most—there was no hope of collecting more from the Trois Couronnes, no certainty that he could get in touch with Britten for more money.

His only ally was the coming darkness; and the unknown man who had warned him. Who would do that?

With Flambaud in a "catch him at all costs" mood, everywhere he might go would be closely guarded. He hadn't the make-up box, and couldn't vary the disguise.

If he could see any chance of proving that Philippe, Raoul, the Count or even Lucille had killed Stella, any wild risk to prove it would be justified—such as breaking into the strong-room again.

If the worst happened he could make Flambaud visit that strong-room.

How had Flambaud discovered where he was hiding?

Mannering sat at the window, watching the darkening sky, touched even then by the magic beauty of the purple dusk. That faded into grey, then darkness. Mannering sat there, forcing himself to go over everything that had happened.

The years had given him a quality that was almost a sixth sense. He knew when he was being followed. He might be fooled once, but not time after time; and he felt quite sure that he had not been followed since his first day here.

He was sure that he had not been followed to the Trois Couronnes.

Only Lorna and Britten had known where he was; could have told the police and the anonymous Frenchman.

Britten.

The thought stabbed.

The night was dark.

A few shops were lighted, but there was little brightness. People sat in the shadows outside the *bistros* and the restaurants in the soft light of lanterns or subdued, coloured electric lamps. The traffic was silent. It was a little after nine o'clock, and Mannering walked along the narrow sidewalk towards the back of the Hôtel Mirage, without any fear of being recognized.

Flambaud might expect him back at the hotel; the danger would come when he began to break in.

He had spent the last lingering hour of daylight and the past hour of darkness thinking about Britten, arguing with himself, saying that he couldn't be right; but was there another explanation? He recalled Britten's odd manner on the telephone, his nervousness, the gun he carried. He remembered that Britten hadn't been able to face Hilda Bennett with the news of Tony's conviction.

There were other things.

Motive?

If Britten had killed Bernard Dale, and his sister had found out, or even suspected, that would be motive enough. Stella had probably gone to see her brother while in London.

Britten knew the Riviera well, had recommended the Mirage, knew estate agents—and also knew the Count and his nephews. He could have come here and sold the Gramercys to the Comte de Chalon, feeling quite secure. Stella might have found out that they had bought those jewels from her brother. Her tension when she had visited the Mannerings might have been due to a sense of guilt— because she knew the truth, and yet admitted only part of it.

Had she told her husband and her brother what she thought, then rushed back to Chalon to be free from the mental torment she suffered in London?

Britten could have followed, killed and silenced her— and pretended to arrive on the Riviera later, to "help" Mannering. When Mannering had telephoned him, he had been away from home.

From the moment he had arrived, he had worked on Mannering's fears. Looking back, it was easy to believe that was deliberate.

Lorna had never been so frightened; perhaps Britten had set out to break her nerve, to convince her Mannering hadn't a hope.

Was it Britten?

Not far along, the crowd had gathered outside the Hôtel Mirage; Mannering could hear the orchestra playing. He did not mix with the crowd, but watched from the other side of the road.

At least seven gendarmes were among the throng outside the hotel, or on the terrace, or on the boulevard near here. Mannering walked past one of them. The man saw him, but obviously did not recognize him.

Mannering crossed the road to the side street; it was very dark.

Two gendarmes were by the side entrance. Once Mannering was inside, the staff of the hotel might recognize him, he would have no chance of brazening it out.

Beyond the entrance, the street was pitch dark; and not far above Mannering's head was a balcony. If he could get on to that, he could climb up to the fourth floor.

He paused in the shadows, listening to the music,

measuring the distance between the ground and that first balcony.

All would go well if the policemen kept looking the other way.

23

BRITTEN

THE two gendarmes were dark silhouettes against the lights of the promenade, but Mannering was against the darkness, at most a shadowy figure. He watched the pair closely, waited until he thought they were facing the other way, then stretched up and gripped the balcony.

He hauled himself up and over.

The window was dark; no one was in the room beyond.

Mannering watched the gendarmes, tensely; they showed no sign that they had seen him.

He looked upwards, at the next balcony. He could reach it by stepping on to a ledge jutting from the wall. It would take more time than the first stage, but it could be done; it was much easier than the house in the rue de l'Arbre.

A little noise wouldn't matter; orchestral music came clearly along the street. The crowd had swelled so much that Mannering could see some of them at the end of the road.

Mannering started up.

In five minutes, he was below the balcony on the fourth floor. He paused. He had nothing to fear from the watching police, little to fear from anyone until he forced his way into Britten's room.

Would Britten be there?

He stretched up, gripped the bottom edge of the balcony, and drew himself up. A minute later, he stepped into a fourth floor bedroom; in a few seconds he was at the door. He listened, heard no one outside, and opened the door.

The lift gates clanged as he stepped outside.

The liftman stepped on to the landing, but didn't glance his way. Two women, smartly dressed, came hurrying towards Mannering. They passed him, one with a half smile.

He reached Britten's room, and listened again; he heard no sound. He took out the picklock, and forced the door.

There was no light.

He closed the door and waited in the little lobby; there was a possibility that he had been seen by a maid, even the liftman. No one approached, no alarm was raised. He didn't lock the door, but stepped into the bedroom, closed that door, and switched on the light.

Everything was as he might expect it to be.

Mannering went to the wardrobe and began to go through Britten's pockets. He found nothing that supported the suspicion which had become almost a certainty—but certainty built on reasoning which might fall down.

He went through all the clothes; two suit-cases; a brief-case. He still found nothing that helped. He stopped, and lit a cigarette. He had taken the wild chance of getting here—and simply lost time. He should have gone to the villa—challenged the Count, Philippe, any of them.

He heard footsteps—and moved swiftly towards the balcony.

The footsteps stopped.

If Britten came in, what would be the right thing to do? Question him? Let him know of the suspicions? That would be crazy; Mannering needed proof, had to have proof.

There was a sharp tap at the door; another; a third.

The man outside did not go away.

Mannering stood close to the french windows, listening. Although the sound of music floated up from the street, he heard a different sound—of metal on metal at the door. Someone was picking the lock.

He heard it click back.

On the balcony he peered into the room, ready to dodge back out of sight at any moment. The light of the passage showed; and against it, the silhouette of a man. The man came in quickly, closed the door, and then whispered in French:

"Now I have simply to wait."

It was Philippe Bidot.

Mannering heard the scrape of a match; there was a flash, then a red glow as Philippe lit his cigarette. He hadn't come on any friendly errand, or he wouldn't have broken in, and most certainly would not have waited in the darkness.

Why should he lie in wait for Britten?

Mannering could find out why; or he could wait until Britten came, listen, perhaps have everything he needed.

He waited.

Smoke from Philippe's cigarette drifted tantalizingly towards him. The orchestra seldom stopped playing, then only for a few minutes.

Philippe put out his cigarette and lit another.

Mannering kept easing his legs, moving cautiously, alert all the time.

In a lull in the music, he heard a key scrape in the lock of the outer door. The door opened wide. Britten came in briskly, and put on the light at once. It flashed out, through the open french window and past Mannering, then lost itself against the darkness.

Britten gave a startled gasp: then:

"What—what are you doing? Put—put that gun away!"

"Oh, no, my friend," said Philippe softly. "I am likely to shoot you with it, if you try to run, or even"—Mannering could imagine the shrug—"even if you lie to me. Just move back against the wall."

"I don't understand ! Why are you here? How did——"

"Oh, I broke in because I wanted a little talk with you," said Philippe. "The answers to one or two questions are important. How long have you and my uncle, M. le Comte, been working together—you as thief, he as buyer of stolen jewels?"

"You must be crazy !" Britten grated.

"Oh, I am not crazy. I know what has happened this time. I know you stole the Gramercys and killed Dale. I know that you framed your friend, Tony Bennett, and would let him hang for you. I know that my uncle was angry because you brought the stones to him so quickly—but you had to, didn't you, because it was not safe for you to keep them in England—especially with the clever John Mannering likely to look for them."

"Mannering—Mannering must have——" Britten began weakly.

"We will have no lies," said Philippe. "These things I know, because I heard you and my uncle discussing them, an hour or two ago. I was hiding in the room where you talked. I drove here ahead of you—the police were in the grounds of the villa, so I could not wait there to discuss this. I do not know which of you killed Stella— my uncle, or you."

"I—I didn't kill her !" denied Britten tautly. "Why— why should I? It was your uncle, he——"

"Go on," said Philippe softly. "Be very careful what you say."

"He must have flown from London without letting anyone know, he——"

"Oh, my poor, foolish friend," said Philippe, and there was mockery in his voice. "He did not fly to Chalon before you—you were here first. I am quite sure that you actually used the knife on Stella. I did not know whether you and my uncle worked together—but had you done so, would you have suggested that he actually *used* the knife?"

Britten said breathlessly: "You're guessing. I didn't——"

"Oh, come," mocked Philippe. "Why don't you admit the truth—that you killed her? You flew on the next plane after her, didn't you? You have accomplices here, besides the Count. One sent a telegram in Mannering's name, saying that Stella must return to Chalon at once. The police found the telegram in her handbag," Philippe went on. "Lucille wheedled *that* information out of a sergeant. Also I heard you say to the Count that the telegram couldn't fail to make the police suspect Mannering. It didn't fail in one sense. Stella came, and you killed her. Afterwards, you were busy trying to frame your own friend, Mannering—the man whom you feared would discover the truth if he were allowed to work without interruption.

"Not knowing what I know about him now, I hindered him, but—the truth has come out," Philippe went on gently. "When I saw you and my uncle together yesterday, I began to suspect the truth. You had to discuss this with him because you did not know what he was likely to say to the police. You were afraid that he might not be able to deceive Flambaud."

"You're making all this up! You——"

"Oh, no," said Philippe. "One of your accomplices here in Chalon is a man who would work for a thief but not for a murderer. He and Lucille have talked. He told her that you were informing the police that Mannering was also le Brun; and that he was at a certain hotel. That told me how you were betraying a friend. Could I need more proof that you were a rogue?"

Britten didn't speak.

"Only a little while ago, one of your men tried to kill Mannering, by running him down," said Philippe. "I have been told about that, too. But things did not go your way, did they?"

"Philippe, listen," said Britten in a different, eager voice. "Your uncle is wealthy. He knows what happened but he daren't say so, because he has so many stolen things in the strong-room. All of us can work together. Raoul will get over it. He——"

"Raoul will not get over it," corrected Philippe. "He is—he has always been an honest man. He had no idea that you and my uncle were dealing in stolen jewels and *objets d'art*. He would never countenance villainy. He is keeping quiet now only because he thinks he can find out who killed Stella best that way. Once he knows, he will tell the whole truth about the Count. And my uncle—he has salved his conscience for years by giving paltry alms to the poor. I've tried to do more, but—no matter!" Philippe became brusque. "Tell me how Stella discovered that you were the murderer. What made her so certain that you were compelled to murder her?"

Britten didn't speak.

"It is so little to answer," Philippe said softly. "How did she find out?"

Britten said savagely: "When I went to see your uncle at the hotel in London, Stella heard us talking about it. It was after the Count had made her tell him that she had been to see Mannering. Afterwards the Count told Mannering that Stella had told him that there was a risk of Mannering finding the strong-room, although Mannering, the fool, told me everything ——"

It was easy to imagine the dread in Britten's mind; understand his viciousness; but Mannering kept on the balcony, without making a sound.

"We—we must make a deal, Philippe," Britten went on in a shrill voice. "Where are the jewels? Did Mannering take them? Or who——"

"It must have been someone else," Philippe said easily. "I could certainly never tell the police that I suspected Mannering. He is just a detective, and this time did not have so much luck. But he will agree, I think, that in the end he had enough. I——"

He broke off.

Mannering felt the sudden pitch of tension, then heard the roar of a shot. A dark shadow appeared on the balcony; then Britten came, staggering. Behind him was Philippe, gun posed.

"Hold it!" Mannering shouted. "Don't shoot!"

He struck Britten as he went forward, and the man slumped back, then crumpled up. He fell almost at Philippe's feet. Philippe stood by the french windows, gun slowly drooping, mouth agape.

Then:

"You—with *Mannering's* voice. You *are* one and the same. And you were there all the time! But the police will come because of the shooting. Hurry! I shall tell Flambaud about Britten, all will be well, but get rid of that disguise. Hurry!"

Philippe was already rushing to open the door.

"You understand, m'sieu," said Flambaud, two days later, "that we do not all work like your Scotland Yard. I was aware that an Englishman had killed Mme. Bidot because a servant heard her talking to an Englishman.

There was also the telegram. I did not know then that Britten was already in Chalon. He pretended to come much later, and——" Flambaud shrugged. "I did not check that, in time.

"Now, I know everything," he boasted. "Some I can prove, some I guess, some—what is your phrase?" he asked, and gave a little grin. "Ah, I remember—off the record! For what a policeman knows but cannot prove does not go before the courts, does it?"

Mannering murmured: "No."

"When Britten learned you were coming to Chalon, he had a warning sent to Philippe Bidot to be especially careful because there might be a visitor to the villa. Philippe heeded the warning; now, he says that he hoped to catch the thief red-handed. When he failed, he thought that you were the thief, and was foolish enough to persuade your wife to go with him, hoping you would admit the truth to get her back. Is that so?" Flambaud flashed.

"Philippe?" asked Mannering, as if shocked. "Impossible. You must be guessing!"

"So you do not intend to give evidence," grumbled Flambaud. "What can a policeman do without evidence? But there is a grave matter not yet settled. Many of the Count's jewels have been stolen—including the Gramercys. However, the Count remains wealthy—and Philippe will inherit much of his money one day, so he will have plenty with which to help his poor. Raoul will remain in business." Flambaud paused, then flashed again: "Do you know where those jewels are, m'sieu?"

"I wish I did," said Mannering sadly.

Flambaud shrugged non-committally, and left the hotel room a few minutes afterwards.

Mannering lit a cigarette, and strolled out on to the balcony. He looked down at the terrace. Lorna and

Lucille were sitting in the shade. He saw Lorna laugh, as if nothing had happened.

It was easy to laugh.

Tony Bennett had been reprieved at the last minute; there would be a re-trial.

The Count had made a full statement, and was under arrest.

Britten had also made a statement, when he had come round. He swore that he had not meant to kill Bernard Dale. But undoubtedly he had meant to take the Gramercys and to have Tony framed for the burglary. He had phoned Tony and attacked him, to destroy his alibi. Mannering wasn't sure how far that was true, but it hardly mattered.

Even Bristow had sent a telegram of congratulation.

Now, Mannering was alone in the room, taking the jewels out of the light-fitting. He parcelled up the jewels, addressed them to Flambaud, carried them downstairs and out by a side door. He posted them at the nearest post office, then strolled towards the sea road and the hotel terrace.

He was thinking of Philippe and Lucille, wondering whether Philippe would take chances to help others, remembering how once Philippe's eyes had shown laughter instead of fear—when Mannering had made it clear that he thought Philippe would be scared by the threat of telling the police about his uncle's strong-room.

Lorna and Lucille were on the terrace.

Lorna's eyes lit up when she saw him, and Lucille jumped to her feet.

"I have been waiting until you came, John. Now I must go to the villa, where Philippe is waiting for me."

Mannering said gravely: "Never keep Philippe waiting, he's an impatient young man."

Lucille laughed, shook hands, and hurried off to the velocipede. She sat on it, started the engine, then waved to them and drove off into the stream of traffic.

Arm-in-arm, the Mannerings went into the hotel.

THE END